THE DEATH MAN

The hardest of men went in fear of Ford, the bounty hunter, who had earned the name The Death Man. Yet even Ford was not infallible — when he killed the wrong man, he found that he was being sought himself by the feared Frank Ambler. Their deadly game covered great distances and was twisted with violence and treachery. At last, Ambler tracked his quarry into an arid land that was a fitting arena for the deadly showdown.

Books by Lee F. Gregson
in the Linford Western Library:

THE MAN OUT THERE
THE STOREKEEPER OF SLEEMAN
LONG AGO IN SERAFINA
SEASON OF DEATH
BRAID

LEE F. GREGSON

THE DEATH MAN

Complete and Unabridged

LINFORD
Leicester

First published in Great Britain in 1992 by
Robert Hale Limited
London

First Linford Edition
published 1997
by arrangement with
Robert Hale Limited
London

British Library CIP Data

Gregson, Lee F.
The Death Man.—Large print ed.—
Linford western library
1. English fiction—20th century
2. Large type books
I. Title
823.9'14 [F]

ISBN 0–7089–5044–2

Published by
F. A. Thorpe (Publishing) Ltd.
Anstey, Leicestershire

Set by Words & Graphics Ltd.
Anstey, Leicestershire
Printed and bound in Great Britain by
T. J. Press (Padstow) Ltd., Padstow, Cornwall

This book is printed on acid-free paper

1

MARGE McLUSKEY'S it was, a rooming house in Lefabor, not much of a town and by its peeled appearance, not much of a rooming house either.

Marge herself was in the kitchen standing at her worn bench, beginning to prepare a mid-day meal when, at a sound, she glanced up and, through the half-curtained window, saw Mace walking a tired horse into the dry yard, horse and rider powdered liberally with white alkali dust, and Mace himself with a two-day growth of dark whiskers. Marge murmured:

"Oh Christ. Him. It ain't never good news this bastard brings." She stood still, a familiar hollow sensation in her stomach, drying her hands on her apron, staring through the flecked glass at Mace, knowing that he must have

1

seen her watching him.

He swung down quite stiffly as might a rider who has come a good long distance without enough rest, and stood for a moment or two glancing around the yard. When his eye fell on the trough he led the chestnut across to it, and while it stretched its neck and began to drink, took off his old hat, dipped it in alongside the horse's muzzle and tipped the contents over his own head. He waited for the horse to finish drinking, then led it to a rail in the shade near the barn and hitched it there. When he came back across the hard-packed yard towards the kitchen she went out on the porch and unsmilingly tossed him a rough towel.

"Dry down. I don't want you comin' in here drippin' all over." She went back inside. When he came in she wordlessly took the dampened towel from him. She knew that Mace was widely considered a dangerous man but she was not afraid of him; not any more and not right now, for sure, for she could tell — feel — that Mace had a lot on his mind, with a pinched look that said maybe he had come to this place only ten strides ahead of some harassing demon. When he stood only a yard away from her she wrinkled her nose and told him he stank.

"So I stink. I rid a hunnert an' forty mile in this Goddamn' heat in no time to speak of, an' a-purpose to warn your man. So I stink." He moved his head, indicating the upper floor. "He up there?"

"He's there."

"How is he?"

She shrugged narrow shoulders. "Who can ever tell? He ain't drunk so he ain't shoutin' nor bustin' nothin' nor bangin' on the floor for nothin', so I'd say he's still in a reasonable frame o' mind, mebbe settin' up there on his own, playin' solitaire. But I don't know for sure how he is, so was I you, I'd knock first." Mace looked at her sourly and went on through into the passageway that led to the stairs, thinking that

3

Marge McLuskey had a splendid little body but a too-smart mouth. She called after him: "Warn him about what?" Mace did not bother to answer. She did hear him call out to Cully to let him know who it was coming upstairs, and there was a murmuring of voices and then a door closed. Marge drew a long breath and went back to her bench and the food she had been preparing.

Not many minutes elapsed before there sounded an urgent clumping of boots coming down the stairs; Cully, gaunt, with a wispy moustache, was first into the kitchen but Mace was not far behind him. Marge raised her dark eyebrows. Without preamble, Cully, in his high-pitched voice said:

"Get some o' my stuff together."

"What in hell's got into you?"

"Look, *do* it, will yuh?" Cully said. His face was unnaturally pale and though he was often sharp with Marge she could see that this time it was because he was shit-scared about something, and whatever it might be,

4

Mace had fetched it to him.

"Where are you goin'? What do you need? Clothes, food, what?"

"Yes! Bloody clothes! Bloody food! Some'ing that'll keep good." To Mace he said: "We'll want extra canteens. There's some in the barn." They went out and across the yard. "An' yuh'd best get a-hold of a fresh animal from somewheres," Cully remarked when he got a look at the chestnut. "How far behind is he, yuh reckon?"

"Can't tell for sure. Could be a day. Could be less."

"Less? Jesus wept!"

"Yeah, well nobody's right certain jes' where he's at, any time. But the word I got was that he was comin' here fer one purpose an' we was it."

Mace got himself a fresh mount from the Lefabor livery. At a price. Word gets about, especially if it is news that is not good and the portents are even worse. Any other time he would have shoved four inches of pistol barrel in the liveryman's mouth. He thought he might do so yet, but it would have to wait. When they got back into Marge's kitchen they found she had hustled about and got Cully's warbag all ready, and his bedroll; and into a gunny sack she had wrapped and put some cold roasted beef and some chunks of coarse brown bread, bacon and beans and coffee, and unasked, she had found an extra box of shells for his Colt. Mace went out again and lost no time in taking saddle and blanket off the chestnut and hoisting it up onto the bay from the livery. In the kitchen Marge stared at Cully, fingers of one hand at her thin neck.

"How do you *know* it's Ford?"

"Mace is sure of it."

"Mace ain't got the brains of a sick blowfly."

"He's sure, Marge. It's Ford right enough."

"If he's comin' for the both of you, it must be about somethin' from a time back. It must be about Colorado."

"It don't matter a shit what it's

about. Ford ain't never concerned over wheres an' whys an' what-have-yous; an' ordinary jurisdiction an' boundaries don't mean nothin' to him. He's a bounty hunter, no more, no less, no interest in what it's for, just so he picks up the money."

"Dead or alive," she said quietly. Cully looked at her, then away. "How far back is he? Does Mace that knows everything know that?"

"No. Well, mebbe less'n a day."

She felt as though she had been punched in the stomach.

"Where will you go?"

"Best yuh don't know that. If he comes here — if Ford comes here — tell him you an' me had an argyment an' yuh threw me out, bag an' bedroll."

"I'm sure he'd believe that right off an' go quietly on his way."

"Tell him what yuh like, but if yuh don't know where we've gone yuh can't tell him that."

"If he does come, I sure as hell hope *he* sees it that way! Here." She handed

him his warbag and then his bedroll.
"Take 'em. I'll fetch the sack out."

Within three minutes of that, they
were up and heading out. Marge went
straight back into the house, not even
wanting to know in which direction
they were pointing.

★ ★ ★

Come sundown they were close upon
the town of Galen near the hook of
the Paradine River, and Mace reckoned
they had made good time considering
the badly broken terrain they had had
to traverse. Along the way they had
encountered no other riders, though
once, in the smoky distance, they
had observed cowboys chousing strays
through brushlands, but that activity
had been nearly two miles away. They
had watched their back-trail assiduously
but had detected no movement there;
not that it meant much, for in country
such as this, a man skilled in such
matters would have had no difficulty in

8

trailing them while contriving to remain out of sight himself.

So now at last they hauled up, and from a gentle rise of ground, in the blue evening, saw that down in the town, lamps were coming on. His horse skewing, stepping sideways, tossing its head, Mace said:

"So what now? Do we risk it, go on down?"

Cully, one gloved hand rubbing along his sharp jawbone, did not answer at once because he himself was not at all certain what they ought to do. Sure, they could make camp and, come sunup, give the town of Galen a wide berth and continue to strike south-west; or they could go on in, put up somewhere and thus spend what felt as though it might be a cold night in comparative comfort; but in so doing, mark their trail plainly for a man such as Ford to follow. Mace, with all the riding he had done recently, looked fit to fall out of the saddle and even Cully, tense as he felt, was tired; tired and angry and in need of a better meal than could be had in a cold camp, so he made up his mind.

"Come on. We want some decent chow an' a few hours' sleep. We can be out o' this dump again long afore sunup."

Mace needed no persuasion. Nonetheless they took their time and entered Galen unobtrusively, leaving their horses at a livery, taking a room apiece at the Galen Palace Hotel and eating their way through a substantial meal. They attracted no more than a glance or two, a couple of trail-dusty hard-noses on their way from no-one-knew-where to some place unspecified, itinerants who were not untypical of travellers through this town. After their meal and a couple of shots of rye that turned out to be not too bad considering the looks of Galen, they felt somewhat better and even a touch more confident.

When they went tramping upstairs only one lamp was lit and burning low in the upper passageway. Cully halted at his own room, went in, Mace continued on to his, let himself in and had crossed to the lamp to turn it up when Ford said:

"Leave it, boy. Stand still. Lift the Colt out, careful, put it on the cot. Don't turn yet." There was the clear, sharp sound of a pistol being cocked.

"Who are yuh?" Mace said, his voice going up. "How the hell did yuh git in here?" Slowly, he laid the big Colt on the cot.

"Shut your mouth." It was a hard, firm voice, but not loud. "Where's Cully? In his room?"

"He's there." Mace's voice had dropped right away. He had known from the start who it was, all right, and his whole body was slick with sweat and he wanted to sit down before his legs maybe gave out under him.

"We'll go there. Walk ahead of me. Now."

Quite carefully, Mace turned. The

light was very poor, but there he was, a tall thin man with a long dark moustache and eye sockets that were pits of darkness, with glittering centres. His clothing was old and none too clean; he was wearing a black hat with a stiff brim, a loose jacket over a buttoned vest, and in his right hand he held very firmly a long pistol, its great eye fixed unmovingly on Mace. Just looking at this tall man, Mace knew better than to argue or to try delaying him, so led him out and along the dim passage to Cully's door.

"What do I say?" mumbled Mace.

"You'll think of something," Ford said softly.

Mace rapped on the door.

"Cully? It's me. Gotta talk. It can't wait."

"Come on in then," called Cully.

Mace went first. Cully, in bright lamplight, was in the act of replacing his .44 Colt in the holster now hanging by its shellbelt from a bedpost. When he saw the man following Mace in and when he saw Mace's expression, at first Cully froze.

"Jesus Christ!"

Then in the shock of the moment Cully made the mistake that Mace had almost prayed he would not make; he stepped to one side very fast, his back to the window, still gripping the pistol, bringing it to bear.

Mace was immediately bumped aside as Ford moved in, and like the shout of doom in the confined space, his big Colt boomed, blue smoke billowing, and Cully, hit fair and square, was thumped backwards; and when the second thunderous shot came — Mace by now on his hands and knees — Cully was again hit hard and this time fell back against the window. The glass creaked, then crunched as his full weight came against it and then Cully was gone out of a room that was filled with blue smoke and the acrid stench of burnt powder and still reverberating with the sounds of the two explosions.

"Get up," Ford said to Mace. They had been inside this room for about seven seconds.

Cully's spectacular fall into the street from the upper floor of the Palace Hotel, had not surprisingly fetched a number of people out, but when Ford came out of the front door of the hotel walking Mace in front of him, they all kept their distance. Ford himself scarcely glanced towards the body of Cully lying bloodily in lamplight spilled from the Palace windows amid shards of glass, but walked on by, directing Mace towards the livery. When shortly afterwards they came out of there, Ford and Mace were mounted and leading Cully's horse with its saddle on. Near Cully's body, they paused. There was a sheriff in Galen by the name of Foster, a man of sixty-five whose knee joints cracked when he walked, and by this time he was there too.

"What in the name o' God's goin' on here?"

"Sheriff," Ford said, "my name's

14

Ezra Ford. This man here is named Mace," and pointing, "and that one on the ground in front of you was called Cully. They are both felons for whom the State of Colorado has had reward money posted these three years past."

"An' you're a bounty hunter, Ford. That it?"

Ford ignored that. He said:

"I'd appreciate a couple of the boys giving me a hand to put Cully on his horse." He swung down, gaunt face, long spidery legs.

"How come he's finished up dead?" Foster asked.

"He was all set to shoot. I shot first. Ask Mace."

Foster rubbed at white stubble, looked towards the man still mounted, whose wrists, he now noticed, were manacled. Mace looked starkly back at Foster and nodded jerkily.

"There's Cully's gun over there," said Ford. "It came out with him." He moved to Cully's body, looking about him, but nobody made as though to help him. Ford shrugged, stooped, and with astonishing strength got hold of Cully and lifted him up. For a few moments he appeared unsteady with the weight of his burden, but then he made one big, grunting effort and got the dead man up and flopped over the saddle. The horse moved but Ford quickly steadied it, making soothing noises. Everybody stood silent, watching, while Ford, fetching a lariat from his own horse, and protecting the belly of Cully's horse with the man's own bedroll, lashed the wrists and ankles of the corpse, passing the rope under the horse, drawing it firmly enough but not so tight as to cause the animal discomfort. There was plenty of rope so he looped it around several times, then brought an end up and hitched around the saddle horn. When he had finished doing that and was satisfied with it, Ford took a bill from a pocket of his levis and gave it to Foster. "That's for the hotel window. Pass it on. I wouldn't want it said that damages weren't paid for." He swung up into his saddle.

"Yuh pullin' out o' here at this hour?"

"Nothin' wrong with the night," said Ford. "I prefer to move at night."

So he departed from Galen with his prisoners, one alive, one dead, and soon all three were swallowed up in the darkness out beyond the edge of the town.

When, finally, he got to where it was he was going, he was riding easy, having packed them, Cully and Mace, both dead, across a lot of inhospitable country, until he brought them to this marshal at Plateau. The marshal, Givens his name was, had no way of knowing how long Ford had been towing them, so stood well back, sniffing tentatively.

"They're not too ripe yet," said Ford in his hard, deep voice. "Not too bad. The flies, they're sou'-western flies the boys brought with 'em, all that way."

Givens squinted at him but could read no hint of levity in Ford's expression.

"Yuh'd best walk 'em 'round the back," he said, "flies an' all."

2

BY some it was firmly held that he was a Missourian, by others that he had been raised in North Carolina. Someone in Kansas who claimed to have known near kin of his, said for sure that he was really from Kentucky; but a peace officer in Tucson, Arizona, spat in the dust of the street when Ford's name was mentioned. "Carolina, Missouri, Kentucky? Not so, friend. Not so. He was born an' bred in a small town in Hell, Ford was, an' then up he come on this here earth with the smell o' brimstone still on him." That was not so, of course, certainly not the part about the brimstone, but people who had passed close to him had been aware that indeed there was a strange odour about him; it was not readily identifiable, but came close to the smell of deep, dank earth.

There were indeed differing views on Ford, offered by diverse people. A woman in the town of Levine recalled him from years ago as one of a group of men who had played stud with her brother and certain others in the kitchen of their house in Boise, Idaho. "Bony, vulture of a feller he was as I recall. I didn't think he was nothin' special." Another woman, the wife of a homesteader forty miles from Tucson, was not at all attracted to Ford either. "Knowed my man from somewheres, Ford did. God knows where. Come twice, three times, an' I can tell you I was glad to see the narrer back o' him every time. Didn't talk up none, not while I was there. Mumblin' in a corner mostly. Don't know what Ed seen in him or what business he had with him 'cause he'd never say. That Ford had old clothes, too, all dark; an' he was rank. On'y thing about Ford that looked good was the horse he come on, an' the cleanest thing about him was the damn' great pistol he had. You could see it when his coat come open, all oiled an' such." So it was clear that while there were those who had no time at all for Ford, there were others with whom the bounty hunter could sit down and not have to watch his back. But they were reckoned to be few and far between. And wherever he might have come from or whomever he counted as friend, Ford seemed not to belong in any particular place, for by his nature and by the uncertainties of his chosen calling, he was a man who, as time went on, kept almost constantly on the move.

Anybody and everybody across a big spread of country knew his name and what it had come to mean, but still the majority of them could not have said with certainty what he looked like. Tales of his activities, however, had enjoyed wide currency. How many of the stories were apocryphal it would have been next to impossible to say, since, over time, the borders of truth and fantasy tend to be absorbed, insidiously, one into the other. He could vanish for long periods, as though he might have some special bolt-hole that nobody else could ever know about. However, there were some certainties, some irrefutable facts about Ford and where he had been and what he had done. For example, against all bets on the matter at the time, he had tracked Emmet Case, the Alabama killer, deep into the baking badlands, and weeks later had brought Case's body into the yard of the Cannon marshal, shot twice in the chest, the two bullet holes two inches apart. In the environs of El Paso he had cornered Kel Burdett and Will Fayne, Burdett dead and Fayne slightly wounded, and reaped a total reward of $7,500 for his ultimate one hour's labour. Then, presented with the option of pursuing Edward Lacey or Reefer Hall, he had chosen to travel a considerably longer distance to bring in Hall, for a higher price, remarking that he had made his calculations with care and would not contemplate working for less than ten dollars an hour.

Ford was thought of poorly enough in some quarters at the best of times, but there had occurred in his activities a change, a strange watershed which brought with it suspicion and then a totally chilling fear. Few people knew it then, but this was the direct result of his experience with a man named Sprague.

Ford had come up with Sprague at an old mine shack in Latrobe Canyon and had picketed his horse and gone forward afoot very quietly, on sandy going. Ford had been tired, for it had been a long haul, the last leg of it, prompted by the thought that he had not wanted to risk Sprague's slipping away on him as he had done earlier, and thus have the $5,000 bounty evaporate. There had been a definite risk that his man would be watching and waiting for him. Nonetheless Ford had pressed on with his stealthy approach and when, pistol drawn, he had kicked the door open, Sprague, caught flat-footed at the pot-bellied stove, had been in the act of pouring a cup of coffee.

Ford had said: "Put it down easy, then turn your back an' raise your hands over your head."

Sprague, heavily-whiskered, raw-eyed, stinking to high Heaven, had done it without once opening his mouth, and Ford had relieved him of the old Colt he had been wearing, and then had the man turn so that he could manacle him. It had gone well. At that point Ford had believed that his decision to move in on his man before sundown was still a good one, for through it, he had secured Sprague swiftly, made quite certain that he could not get out of the canyon and so further out again into broken, ravaged country where it might have been next to impossible to get him boxed a second time. Later, Ford had had reason to doubt his decision not to hold back. Hours later, the pot-belly still glowing. Sprague stretched out on a bunk, manacled hands resting on his chest, Ford, propped in a corner, his pistol on the floor nearby, had thought he would have given half the bounty right then in exchange for an easy sleep. His eyes had been burning, his head throbbing with weariness and he had long since admitted to himself that it would have been smarter to have made a solitary, fireless camp near the mouth of the canyon and to have closed in on Sprague just before sunup. Yet with a firm will Ford had forced himself to watch through the night, and an hour before the eastern sky lightened he had risen stiffly to his feet and fed more wood into the stove. He had fetched bacon from his own supplies, and coffee, and cooked their breakfast, and then, his hand ringing with weariness, had got the horses saddled and the surly Sprague mounted, and had set out from the canyon's mouth, the horses at a walk,

Ford trailing the still-manacled Sprague by five yards.

Sprague, of course, had had the desperate cunning of a man who had been cornered, humiliated, and whose destiny was now fixed, whose future held but one awful finality. So Sprague had known that unless, during the coming hours, he could create for himself one good chance at Ford, he was done for; and he had needed no special powers of perception to realize that Ford was desperately tired. Somewhere along the line, Ford, the infallible, had miscalculated, made a mistake, had pushed too hard after his quarry and was now paying a price for it.

Suddenly, raspingly, Ford had said: "Turn around. Face ahead."

The bastard, Sprague had thought. The bastard doesn't sleep. Yet he had still believed that time itself was his ally; that and the blazing sun. For the day's heat had been rising as they had left Latrobe Canyon behind them, wending in and out between grainy, reddish rocks and had settled to a steady, unhurried yet mile-eating pace, Ford keeping his constant trailing distance, for though Sprague had been manacled, Ford had still viewed that distance as his margin of safety.

They had ridden on under the unforgiving sun, Sprague not turning his head any more but occasionally heeding a low call from the man riding behind, to change direction, head for some fresh landmark in the shimmering distance. But Sprague had cradled the knowledge that they had a hell of a long way still to go, and that every sapping mile of it must eat at Ford's awareness to a much greater degree than his own.

It had been at the waterhole near Red Bluffs that Sprague had made his move; though it had not been a chance easily presented, for dog-tired or not, Ford, if nothing else, was a professional.

"Stay up 'til I tell you," Ford had

said, and Sprague had heard the creaking of leather behind him as the bounty hunter had dismounted.

First, Ford had replenished the canteens from the none-too-clear water, had led his own horse down to the rippling edge and allowed it to drink. The other mount, Sprague's, restless through being held back, had tossed and whickered but Ford had insisted that Sprague stay where he was, and not until he thought the time was right did he motion for him to get himself down out of the saddle and see to the welfare of the horse. Ford himself had moved further away and, scarcely taking his attention from Sprague, had removed his firm-brimmed hat and kneeling, sluiced water over his own head and face. Still watching Sprague carefully, he had walked back to the horses, water still streaming down him. Sprague had been kneeling at the water's edge, also slopping water on his face and now had begun to get up, but part-way up had again gone down on one knee, both chained hands pressed to his middle.

Ford had reached in under the loose jacket and drawn the pistol.

"Get up."

Sprague, still kneeling, had begun shaking his head slowly from side to side.

"Can't. Can't do it, Ford. It's my belly."

Ford had come forward and placed the cold hard barrel of the pistol against the left cheekbone of the kneeling man.

"Get up."

Sprague had not even answered, his head sinking forward onto his chest, clenched hands still pressed into his middle.

Whether the buzzing weariness in Ford's head had been the reason or not, Ford would never know, but it had been at that moment that he had allowed his guard to go down, had slid the pistol smoothly back into its holster and leaned in to help Sprague. How Sprague, although aware of the opening through Ford's reflection in the water, had managed to turn and rise so fast would also be a matter to torment Ford's mind, asleep and awake, ever afterwards; but somehow Sprague had, and moreover had got the short chain of the irons over Ford's hat and then across the back of his neck, and so, both men clenched hard together, they had lurched and staggered, wrenching at one another, bellowing, gasping, dust rising around them, the horses backing off, wide-eyed, heads working. The unyielding, tautened chain across his neck had caused Ford to cry out hoarsely, once. Together they crabbed awkwardly, ploughing into the water, shoving, pulling, yelling obscenities, Sprague the fresher of the two, banking on Ford's lack of rest to work in his favour, but reckoning without the man's immense strength, something not apparent when looking at his bony physique. Craggy jaw pressed over one of Sprague's shoulders, Ford had got his big hands to work, punching short but savage jabs in under Sprague's ribs as the fighters staggered this way and that, churning muddied water up around their calves, and at each blow Sprague had gasped; then Ford's hard forehead had snapped sharply forward against Sprague's nose, flooding his eyes, his arms slackening, and the instant that the pressure had relaxed, Ford's long head had been down and out of the manacle trap, wrenching his hat off, and as soon as that had happened Sprague had been as good as cold meat. He had fallen into the water and by the time he had recovered himself, Ford had been up on firm ground once more, the pistol big in his hand. Ford's neck, scored raw by the sawing chain of the manacles had been hurting him badly, his face tight with anger, his deeply-set black eyes glittering. Awkwardly, miserably, Sprague had come sloshing out of the water-hole, his whole attention engaged by the huge black eye of the pistol.

Chest still heaving, Ford had said:

"I ought to be whipped. You're the first bastard ever done that, Sprague, an' you'll be the last."

Even then, Sprague, standing pants and boots sodden, had not understood what was about to happen. Not until Ford had actually raised the pistol in a way that had not simply been covering Sprague but with that hunched intentness which always preceded shooting, had Sprague suddenly realized that he had perhaps only seconds left on earth, that he was into the last hurrying instants of life; yet in a curiously contracted period of time that had seemed an age but had been perhaps a tick of a clock, he had had time to lift his raw, manacled wrists up before his face, his turned-aside, bleeding-nosed face, in a ridiculous and futile act of warding off the inevitable.

"No! For the love o' God, Ford!"

The blast of the big gun had set the horses back-stepping, whickering, the wash of blue smoke had been sharp in Ford's pinched nostrils as Sprague had been punched away abruptly as by a hammer striking his breastbone, to fall back, slapping into the water, setting glass-shard splashes flying; and even after he had twitched convulsively and then gone tightly still, ripples had gone out, widening silently, to the farthest reaches of the pool.

Ford had stood for almost a half minute after he had shot Sprague, still holding the pistol, and in those moments of immense relief had vowed that never again would any man that he had taken be given even the merest whisker of the chance that in his weary carelessness he had given to Sprague.

That marked the beginning of the time when Ford began to bring them all in dead; and it had been from around that time, too, that some had begun muttering about him as The Death Man.

3

THE town was Beauville and the target was the Beauville bank. At ten forty five on a Friday morning, three cloth-masked, shouting men arrived, all armed with long pistols, and in fewer than five minutes they got almost fifteen thousand dollars which they stuffed into a canvas sack they had fetched with them. It was just as they were in the act of leaving that a young woman, unaware of what was happening inside the bank, came around the corner of the building. Startled by the movement to his right, one of the bandits half turned and his gun erupted in a flash and a cloud of blue smoke, and then they were all crowding the light-hitched horses, mounting up, shouting: "Back off! Stay back!" Not until they were at the top of the Main, thrashing the horses madly onward, crouching, trying to reduce themselves as targets, was a shot or two fired in their direction.

People had run towards the woman who had been shot, and another woman, a relative, in great distress, had to be led away. For the wounded girl, however, there was nothing that could be done, and even before they made to carry her inside the bank where it was intended to do whatever they could for her while someone rode the thirty miles to Clavel for a doctor, she died as a result of the big gunshot wound in the side of her head.

Porter, the Beauville sheriff, got up a small posse which, in the event, because people were unaccustomed to such things, took some little while to get moving. It had in fact, gone eleven o'clock before they headed out of Beauville, and Porter was none too pleased. He said that in view of what had happened he needed a lot more luck than that. As it fell out, his luck was not all bad that day, for six miles south of the town, on a brushy flat, they caught one of them because his horse had gone lame and he had been unable to keep pace with his companions. It appeared that neither of them, for they were nowhere in sight, had been prepared to mount him up, double.

Though there could be no certainty that the man they had got was the one responsible for the death of the young woman, and the man himself refused to say anything whatsoever, he was all they had, so it would be his bad luck. It's all about luck, thought Porter, good and bad.

★ ★ ★

He was well chained, so Porter, who was by no means a vindictive man, permitted him some time on a chair in the door-yard, a place where no-one else would be likely to see him. Having failed to impress Porter, a small group of townsmen had long ago dispersed from Main and he did not expect them to come back until either he tried to move Joe Half out of Beauville for trial or the judge came to the town to start the hearing there. But if he had calculated that a considerate act might also help in thawing out Joe Half and maybe start him off talking, he was to be disappointed. The coppery-skinned man sat immobile and without expression, still wearing the black, feathered hat with the snakeskin band, different headgear from that worn by him during the holdup, manacled hands clasped between his knees, his manacled, bootless feet on the ground.

"It would mebbe help yuh, Joe," Porter said, not for the first time, "if yuh was to talk to me. There's bad blood about this. There's real bad feelin' not only here but all through the county. Bad enough that somebody got killed; a lot worse that it was a young woman."

Joe Half's face might just as well

have been chipped out of stone, for it registered about the same degree of animation. Even the man's strange, light blue eyes, set deeply in his high-cheeked, bronze Indian face seemed lifeless.

"It's all very well," Porter said, "fallin' back on that Injun no-talk, but you hear this, Joe; this here set-to ain't the first go at the bank here in Beauville, times bein' what they are, an' that's stuck right in the craw of every man that's still got a dollar or so in it. An' now there's this bad killin' as well. Yuh know that the county an' the bank got a reward out already? Two thousand dollars dead or alive for the other two. An' yuh know what else?" No response, not even a glance in his direction. "I only want one other name from yuh, Joe. I already got one, an' that name's already sent out."

Slowly Joe Half's head turned and his wrong-colour eyes burned into Porter, but still he sat there on the straight-backed chair, silently. Even when Porter asked him if he wanted to know which one of them was now known to Porter and everyone else, Joe Half did not answer. It was like talking to a totem pole. All of them had worn identical blue army fatigue hats and long buff dust coats but had had variously-coloured bandannas pulled up over their noses.

"Feller that had the blue bandanna. When he come out runnin' an' swung up on the horse, two fellers in Gibson's hardware got a good look when the bandanna slipped down. They knowed who he looked like, that hombre. Young buck from Elgin County. Bob Ambler."

Joe Half continued staring back at Porter, his expression unchanging.

"So that's one that won't get away with it," Porter went on doggedly. "So what's the problem? We got you. We'll get Ambler sure as sunup. Do yourself some good, Joe, an' tell us who the third one was."

Joe Half looked away, then stood up,

manacles clinking.

"Come on then," Porter said, shrugging, and took the shuffling man back to the barred cell and locked him in. It had been in his mind to unsettle the prisoner by surprising him about young Ambler, but that too, seemed to have misfired. Anyway, sooner or later they would get Ambler, for those who had identified him said they were certain about the matter. He had been one of the bandits. Well, reasonably certain, because after all it had happened very fast.

When, to Porter's relief, the judge came to Beauville, there also arrived two lawyers and some people from far-off newspapers, and a crowd of sorts did gather outside the jail, but it was not an unruly crowd, largely due to the fact that the town in general was still in a state of shock; and when Porter went out on the boardwalk with his long shotgun cradled in the crook of an arm and told them all to go home, they drifted away without giving him any problems. From among the young bloods he did hire a couple of temporary deputies for the duration of the trial and this show of martial force also had the effect of settling things down and providing at least an illusion of controlled competence. Though he was unable to provide his deputies with badges of office, a compromise was found in that both wore light blue shirts with black string ties, assumed serious expressions and carried an old Winchester apiece, these last furnished by Sheriff Porter out of his limited armoury.

The trial of Joe Half, held in Reefer's barn behind the livery, though conducted in somewhat surprising decorum but in a respiratorily irritating atmosphere of floating straw dust, had a predictable outcome, and the very day following the verdict, some lumber was accumulated, and from where he was in Porter's jail, Joe Half could hear clearly the hammering which meant that gallows from which he was to hang were being constructed.

Porter persisted in his attempts to induce Joe Half to speak about his accomplices but he encountered the now very familiar, quite implacable silence. Only once did the interest of the prisoner seem to be engaged.

"The third one, we'll find him sooner or later. He's the one got the money sack, I reckon." No money had been found in Joe Half's possession apart from a few inconsequential coins. "The other, young Ambler, he don't have no chance now. Like I said, we got the reward promise sent out from Fremont on the telegraph, sent out all over. He's lit out, sure, but already the word is that Ford's on his trail." For an instant Porter believed he had hit a mark. For once there had come a flicker in that stone-eyed gaze, yet so slight and so brief had it been that right afterwards Porter could be by no means certain that he had really noticed it. Nonetheless he pressed what he thought might just be an advantage. "So it was Ambler?" There was no response, but Joe Half, manacled, sitting on the edge of the bunk, swung his long legs up to lie full length, then turned his face to the wall. "Hm," Porter muttered, "audience at an end," and went out of the cell and locked the barred door behind him.

★ ★ ★

Ford had picketed his horse and climbed up in between two great slabs of rock to a place from which the broad, grassy valley lay spread before him. He had with him a small brass spyglass and with it carried out a slow and careful scrutiny of the country before him. There was not a lot of day remaining and he wanted to be quite certain that the man he had been trailing for three days had paused somewhere in this place and was still not aware that he was being followed. After several minutes of intense examination Ford

43

had begun to believe that he had made an unaccountable blunder and that his quarry had spotted him at some stage and had slipped him. The shuddering disc of the glass, cloudy with distance, moved back and forth with the utmost deliberation; it stopped, moved back a touch. There, by God. There he was. The horse had been picketed, the saddle and blanket removed and the rider had made a camp. There was no fire of course. Ford snapped the spyglass shut. He had estimated the distance, and by memorizing a feature of the hilly skyline miles beyond, was quite confident of making his approach in a direct line to where the man was. But he would not move in today. He would rest and he would make his approach an hour before sunup. He always learned from past mistakes.

* * *

Surprisingly, though he had not again raised the matter with his prisoner,

Porter was delivered something of a shock.

"You better be right, old mister Star," Joe Half said. He had a low, guttural way of speaking that Porter had sometimes thought to be overdone, as though the man was trying to sound a lot more Indian than in fact he was. One of Porter's temporary deputies, unasked, had delivered himself of a homily upon the Indian mind for what he had no doubt considered would be Porter's benefit, and among other things had said:

"Now, an Injun, he's different. He's got . . . beliefs, knows things — so he says — hears things on'y an Injun kin hear an see. He lives in a different world from you an' me, Mr Porter."

"What does the other half of Joe Half know an' hear an' see? The part that ain't Injun?"

"It don't work like that, Mr Porter. 'Long as he's got *some* Injun, then he's got different powers."

"Joe Half don't seem all that different

to me," Porter had said, "except he don't talk a lot, an' that's no bad thing in itself."

But now, Joe Half, who did not talk a lot, and in fact in recent days had not wished to say anything at all, had suddenly advised:

"Better be right."

"About what?" asked Porter. "About Ambler?"

The intense, incongruous blue eyes fastened on him directly and unmovingly.

"Yeah, Ambler."

"What does that mean? Yuh sayin' it warn't him?" Joe Half seemed to have slipped back into his earlier state of impenetrable silence. "Joe? that what yuh're sayin'?"

Visibly Joe Half drew himself up and he held his manacled wrists crossed at his middle. He made the merest movement with his head.

"Jesus H. Christ, man! Why didn't yuh say it before?" He might as well have been talking to the wall. Joe Half had again retreated into himself and nothing that Porter could say would induce him to speak again.

Not much more than a half hour later, Porter had to visit him again, first unlocking the manacles that were on his wrists, then relocking them with the prisoner's hands now behind him.

"It's time, Joe," Porter said.

Ten minutes later, Joe Half, having abruptly passed down through the trap, head cocked to one side, was slowly turning on the rope. Inside the jail, on the bunk he had lately occupied, was his black hat with the feather and the snakeskin band. It was all that was left behind of Joe Half.

★ ★ ★

Porter was at the bank, not wanting to sit down, pacing about in the office of the manager, a man named Makin. Makin was saying:

"We'll simply have to send out another telegraph from Fremont explaining about Ambler. About the mistake.

That's if you are quite sure that the Indian wasn't misleading you." It sounded so simple. Perhaps it was, to Makin.

"He made it as plain to me as he was of a mind to, or his nature would let him. But I didn't mistake what Joe was tellin' me. He wouldn't give me no names, an' right at bottom I didn't really expect he would; but he sure did let me know in his own way that we was wrong about Ambler."

Makin shifted uncomfortably in his chair, causing it to creak.

"The witnesses — "

"The witnesses ain't prepared to put money on it no more, neither, which is another good reason for believin' Joe," Porter said heavily. "I've talked again to the damn' witnesses. Listen, young Ambler ain't no saint. In fact he's been a wild young bastard at times; but he ain't been in nothin' like this, Makin, an' we both know it."

Makin steepled his short fingers, sat staring at the top of his desk before again looking up at Porter.

"What more can we do but get it put out on the telegraph?"

"Nothin'," said Porter. "One o' my new-found deputies has had his term extended an' he's already on the way to Fremont, but I reckon it'll be a wasted journey."

"How so?"

"There's a strong rumour that Ford's out lookin' for Ambler."

Makin drew a none-too-steady breath. "Ford."

"So that makes it even worse," said Porter. "It's now some while, I hear, since Ezra Ford fetched in anybody that was anything but dead."

"We can't know for certain that that will happen in this particular case, if indeed Ford does catch up with him."

"Would you like to bet the bank on it that he won't? I know I wouldn't want to bet two bits on it. Ambler ain't in neither this county nor Elgin, that I do know. Now, whether that

was by happenstance or him gittin'
the wheeze that he was bein' sought
after, I don't know. If he did hear
about our damn' witnesses he coulda
lit out to be on the safe side. But
wherever he is an' for whatever reason,
Ford'll catch up with him. That bein'
what I consider a certainty, there's
another thing we better begin thinkin'
about."

"What?" Clearly Makin had not
given this whole matter nearly as
much attention as Porter thought he
ought to have done.

"What about Frank Ambler?"

Makin's pouchy face seemed to sag
and take on the colour of pale dough,
but he said:

"*Frank* Ambler? Frank Ambler hasn't
been near this part of the country, to
my knowledge, for years."

"So. An' do yuh believe that's gonna
continue to be the case if anything bad
should befall his brother? D'yuh think
that? If it's seen that there's been a
mistake?"

"If it . . . Ford. It would be Ford that he . . . " Makin trailed off, sweat shining faintly below his sandy hairline.

"It would be Ford. It would be the so-called witnesses. It would be me. It would be you. It would be anybody at all who'd had a finger in the two thousand dollars. Dead or alive. Nobody in his right senses would want to have to make *explanations* like these to Frank Ambler."

"If he's still living," Makin said, though not with true conviction.

"Well," Porter said, "when this particular can rattles I reckon we'll all find out soon enough."

Makin's tongue probed dry lips and he wanted to look anywhere but at Porter. Without hope, he mumbled:

"This is all supposition. Ford might *not* find young Ambler; and if he *does*, he might also become convinced — be given absolute proof — that the boy was not in it. But if . . . anything *does* happen — "

"Yuh mean if Ford kills him?" Makin

raised his soft hands off the desk, let them fall again.

"If he does, yes, then perhaps Frank Ambler won't even get to hear of it."

"An' that," said Porter, "as well as bein' more supposition, is wishful thinkin' as well."

★ ★ ★

Bob Ambler was nineteen years old but looked to be a couple of years beyond that. High-spirited rather than bad, he had been in his share of scrapes, and then some; though he seemed to have drawn certain lines about what he would do and what he would not do. Yet though he did seem older than his years, he was not so mature when it came right down to it; and making himself scarce when the word came out about the bank at Beauville had been by no means a smart move to make. Now, with this tall, bony, darkly-dressed man here in the odd-looking stiff-brimmed hat which, had it not been for the presence of other appurtenances, would have made him appear to be Amish, it seemed to have been a truly ill-considered, even stupid one. For the second time, the boy said:

"They made a mistake. I wasn't there."

"Then why run?" The voice was firm and hard, clear enough without being overly loud. He was holding a Navy Colt in his right hand.

"Hell, I don't know. It was a loco thing to do, sure, but I heard there was some woman dead there, an' it was my name that was hot in the mouths, an' I reckoned they might be a mite too quick with a rope."

The man's dark eyes registered nothing, neither belief nor disbelief. He was like some cold talleyman checking off responses to a set of listed questions.

"Why do you think they would put your name out if you weren't there?"

"I don't know that. Yuh'd have to ask them that."

"I'm askin' you. Do you know who I am?"

"Yeah, I reckon. You're Ford."

"You ever seen me afore?"

"No. But I know yuh're him. Ain't yuh?"

Ford nodded gently.

"A thousand," he said. "A thousand each. Where's the other one gone?"

"I don't know. I wasn't with nobody else."

"So you said. I hear they did get hold of one other. Some Injun."

"Yuh seem to hear a lot," young Ambler remarked.

"I keep informed," said Ford. "The telegraph is a real boon. It sings of life an' it sings of death. It sings deeds an' it sings names."

"Well, now it's singin' the wrong one," said Ambler.

"You'd never begin to believe how many hombres said 'it wasn't me' when all the time it was."

"Look," said Bob Ambler, "the nearest town to where we are now would be Tanner's Crossing. It's got one o' your damn' telegraphs. Why don't we go there an' you can ask the wire some more questions?"

"Why don't we? Because it ain't needed, that's why," Ford told him. "I know already what word came to me, what name. The word was all about the Beauville bank and the name was Bob Ambler, an' you are him." He backed off three paces. "Get that horse saddled now, boy. We're on our way."

No matter how hard and how long he might curse himself for a fool, young Ambler knew that it would avail him nothing. Ultimately he would have to rely on being able to convince Porter in Beauville itself that he was not the man they ought to be seeking. He knew that he would be wasting his time arguing with Ford.

★ ★ ★

It was past nine at night, a week after the hanging. Porter had walked the length of Main, looked in at the two saloons, walked in and out of a few unlit alleys, been spoken to by the few people he had encountered, had been barked at by sundry dogs in shadowy back lots and now had arrived back at the jail office. In the unkempt, empty lot right next to it the gallows still stood, a mute expression of a civic hope that others might yet be brought to book for the robbery and the needless killing at the Beauville bank.

Porter's left knee, his bad one, had begun to ache as it did sometimes when all his other joints were tired and he himself was feeling somewhat down. Until a few days ago his life as the sole steward of order in the town had been one of comparative peace. It was true that from time to time he had to take a hand in some untidy saloon altercation; and during the past year and a half there had been three unsuccessful attempts at robbery, two at the bank and one at the stage line office, and while these untoward incidents had unsettled the town burghers at the time, there had been in each of them an element of spontaneous randomness, and in one case, outright drunkenness. But in none of them had anyone been hurt. Now, however, thought Porter, here he was at age fifty with a slight though more frequently-recurring ache in his left leg, riding out after killers, comforting — albeit clumsily — the bereaved, sending out messages and then sending out retractions of them because of his being exposed to idiots, and with this ugly, hollow feeling behind his belt buckle which meant that what had begun in Beauville at 10.45 am on an otherwise normal Friday morning, might have a tortuous and dangerous way to run before anybody could say that it was truly over. He had hung Joe Half's old black hat on a peg in the office as an enduring reminder of fragile mortality.

The Beauville jail was a two-storey structure and Porter had his living quarters on the upper floor. Now, he locked up the lower, street door, and turned the office lamp down and went tramping up the narrow, bare wooden stairs. Earlier he had lit a lamp and left it burning low in the room where he ate his meals, and he went there now. As Porter was moving to turn the lamp up, and as he had done elsewhere, with Mace, Ford said:

"Steady." And as Porter made to turn: "Steady!" A pistol cocked.

Porter turned anyway, but slowly, so that there could be no possible misunderstanding.

"How the hell did yuh get in here?"

"Without much trouble," said Ford. "But that's beside the point." He uncocked the gun and holstered it on his left side, high up under his loose-fitting jacket.

"Don't tell me," Porter said wearily, dragging a chair out and sitting down. "Yuh've found young Ambler."

"Was there some doubt in your mind that I would?"

"Where is he?"

"I've got him out back."

Porter stared at him, the gaunt, dark, gangling man who favoured dark clothing, a sinister man, and none too clean. Porter could definitely smell him, a musty, earthy smell like the smell inside an old cave. Porter said:

"If he's alive, well an' good. If he's dead we're all in some real damn' trouble, Ford."

Ford's cadaverous expression did not alter appreciably, though there did seem to be a tightening, a hardening along the jaw. The black, drooping moustache lent to him a certain satanic aspect and his black eyes in their deep sockets bored into Porter. Ford was not the sort of man to pussyfoot around.

"Ambler's dead."

"Christ."

"What's the problem?"

Porter rubbed savagely at his jaw.

"The problem," he said, "is that we got more information because some witnesses changed their bloody minds.

Bob Ambler wasn't at the bank. He just wasn't there. We sent out another telegraph though we didn't think there was much of a chance it would do any good. But why is he dead?"

"He was unlucky," Ford said.

"That's not enough," said Porter, "I need to know — "

Ford cut in sharply: "That *is* enough. Two men, one named, the other unknown, two thousand dollars. Dead or alive. The one with the name that was given is out back, dead. Now I want the money for my work so far."

"It can't happen like that," Porter said.

"It must happen like that," said Ford. "If you put out a name an' the name is wrong, that's none of my concern. It's yours."

Deep down Porter knew that Ford's sharp argument was logical and ought to prevail. He did not know how Makin would see it. Or maybe he did.

"I'll talk with the bank," he said. "I can't do that before the morning."

"No," said Ford. "We'll go tonight, see whoever it is that has to be seen. I've not got time to waste in Beauville." His whole demeanour said there would be no denying him. As for Porter, he thought he would be damn' pleased to be shut of the man.

They carried him into the cell and put him on the floor. There was a good deal of congealed blood, gone black, on the front of his shirt from the two bullet holes on the chest, on the left side, about three inches apart.

"Good shooting," said Porter. "Did he draw?"

"Not entirely," said Ford.

What welled-up in Porter was not pure anger; there was a tincture of frustration and of guilt and rather more of apprehension as well. It would be utterly pointless, he knew, trying to press this bounty hunter further concerning the manner of young Ambler's death. Death. Porter had heard that in some parts of the country Ford had become The Death

Man. Porter himself was not much for fanciful names or cheap saloon drama. He said:

"Yuh know who he is, I take it? This here dead man? Yuh know he's a younger brother o' Frank Ambler?" He had no doubt in his own mind that Ford would have made the connection. Whatever it might have been that had driven him to kill this boy must have been threatening indeed, and powerful. No man, no matter how confident he might be in his own ability, or even how stupid he might be — and Ford was anything but stupid — would lightly discount the threat of Frank Ambler. Or how afraid he might have become. This new thought teased at Porter as he saw Ford staring back at him unemotionally. Maybe Ford had lost it, was past it. Maybe Sprague, in trying for him as Ford had told some he had done, and even though failing, had killed something in Ford himself.

"I did hear some good while back,"

Ford said unexpectedly, "that Frank Ambler is dead."

Heard or hoped?

"Best hope yuh heard right," said Porter. Suddenly he felt very old indeed. Everything bad that had happened to him seemed to have happened during the past week or so. He knew that there would be no deflecting Ford from his determination to be paid at once for the man he had brought in, so Porter made a motion with his head for the gaunt man to follow him, and went out of the cell.

4

RISKING outright rejection he had stood under the scrutiny of her warm honey eyes and right off told her why he was standing there.

Today was the second visit, and the flimsy boxes were assembled just as she had promised. They both sat down and she began to lift out the top bundles and put them on the smooth table.

"Eastern publishers would have paid good money for these, no doubt."

"I know. There have been plenty of offers of course, but for the moment, anyway, I've turned them all down. And it isn't anything to do with money. These photographs were a big part of my father's life. While they remain with me I have something that was very much *of* him."

"I believe I can understand that."

"Not many of the people who wanted to buy them could. In fact I doubt that they would have truly valued them for what they really are. They simply wanted to turn a quick profit. One day, perhaps, I shall make a careful selection, have the very best of them published, all together."

"Your father saw them as a record, a history?"

"Yes. He used to say that, in time, not only would the people vanish but so too would many of the towns; and even those towns which remained and grew would soon enough lose their original character. And the smaller ranches would eventually be swallowed up by bigger ones and their individual character will be lost. After all that happened, no-one would remember; so he wanted to capture as much of it as possible, preserve it, just as it was. Whatever journalists or anybody else might make of it in years to come, this was the reality." She spread the first of the grainy old prints on the table. "Anyway, let's begin, shall we?"

* * *

Ford had left Beauville at once and no-one knew where he had gone. It was one of his periods of disappearance. Though Makin had argued strongly against paying him, he was doing it more out of chagrin arising from their own errors rather than challenging Ford's logic; and Makin had argued thus while knowing that Porter was not with him. Porter knew that whatever might be thought of Ambler being brought in dead and even if there was by now an inescapable conclusion about that, they were bound to honour the payment of the bounty. That was Porter's logic. The appalling fact that the wrong man had been named and so had been brought in, was not Ford's problem.

Since that night many weeks had gone by and there had still been no further word of Ford, no sightings whatsoever. Maybe word had come to him too, as it had come to Porter now, that whatever might have been rumoured to the contrary, Frank Ambler was not dead.

Somehow, the way he was dressed when he appeared at her door, more in keeping with an eastern cattle buyer or railroad manager, well-made suit, looped watch chain, stout brogues, wide brimmed but eastern-looking hat, did not square with the appearance of the man himself. Tall, broad shouldered, with a deeply tanned face that was scarred slightly in places, his eyes were the real incongruity; the colour of gunmetal, while they were capable of smiling when his mouth smiled, occasionally, in more unguarded moments they could be chilling, almost frightening, as though he might be a man haunted by unseen demons. He had made no secret of his purpose, yet he had given her only a half truth. She knew that it was a certain face that he was seeking but he had not told her why, nor had she asked. It was, he thought in his turn, one of the warm things about her, this quiet, unquestioning accommodation of a stranger.

He had been gratified, almost boyish, when he had discovered that so many names had been written on the backs of the photographs, whether of places or of people. All but a few in each bundle were so inscribed.

Occasionally they digressed; it was difficult not to do so, so rich was the hoard. Thriving cattle towns there were, railheads; others, small nondescript communities dating back, some of them, more than a quarter of a century. But there were many subjects other than towns. Here too were huge, dust-smoking herds of cattle on the move, attended by the misty outlines of never-to-be-known horsemen; of chuck wagons, of range crews hunkered at their chow; and of lonely homesteads, sad-eyed women with clinging children standing in black doorways. Impromptu studies too, there were; people climbing down from stage coaches, standing in saloons or sitting on benches in the shade; and there were formal, often self-conscious groups as well, men and women and children in nowhere-places all across the far-flung west.

"Not all of these, in this bundle, were taken by my father," she said. "A few he collected from other photographers. Like this one." It had the name William Bonney written across it in all-but-faded ink.

He studied it. The lantern-jawed, buck-toothed young man was standing alone, his fingers supporting, by the barrel, what seemed to be a Winchester rifle.

"That isn't Bonney," he said. "Did your father know that?"

"Yes."

That in fact was another matter of concern to this man. It was also necessary, by some means, to separate truths from untruths, for nothing in that huge and often lawless land could be taken as cast-iron certain.

She had now come to realize that there was a quite grim intensity about the search he was carrying out. With growing interest she had watched him, then with an uncomfortable apprehension, become drawn into a kind of tension as she saw the way he examined with utmost care the faces, not only of the lone men, but individual faces in each group, yet just as quickly dismissing those whose names were given, setting aside others, unidentified, to be studied again later. From time to time he murmured names, allowing his eyes to linger, as though the woman were not still there in the room with him, as though he might have gone on alone somewhere, down some dark canyon of the mind: "Rudabaugh, Dave Rudabaugh . . . Doc Holliday . . . Frank James . . . Morgan Earp . . . the Clantons, dead . . . Pat Garrett." But plainly the name he sought was not there among them.

The fourth time he visited, the last, there was a bleakness about him, a sense almost of defeat. She had fetched coffee.

"Will you come again, after today? Go through them again, to be certain?"

"No. No, I've intruded here enough." He had picked up his cup but now put it down before it reached his lips.

The picture was clear, taken on a good bright day in a ramshackle town — for some of the wind-burned structures could be distinguished in the background — and the man was standing at the shoulder of a hitched horse, his face turned towards the camera, his expression not quite of surprise, but not of approval either. He was a thin man, could be said to be gaunt, with a black, inverted-horseshoe of a moustache, thick dark brows, and beneath them, deeply-set, small eyes, like black, polished stones. His clothing was old and had the appearance of being none too clean, his black hat, stiff-brimmed, with a round crown like an Amish hat; his shirt was of a lighter shade than the levis he wore, probably light blue, and he wore over the shirt a close-buttoned vest and over that a loose-fitting jacket of some lightweight material that had swung wide as he half turned, and a Navy Colt, its holster held in some kind of sling, plain wooden butt foremost, jutted from under his left arm for a high cross-draw. No conventional shellbelt was worn but the twin, breast-high pockets of his jacket had been reworked with pieces of leather to hold extra loads for the pistol. This was the one. This was him. He knew it before he turned the photograph over slowly, hoping with unreasonably blind hope for an inscription; and for one agonizing moment he thought that there was none. Yet when he looked again closely, there it was, in pencil, barely legible now, and he read it aloud, softly:

"E. Ford."

She had come around the table to his shoulder, sensing relief, elation, triumph and something else she could not define.

"Is that it? Is that him?"

"That's him."

She had to ask it now, even though she had promised herself that she would not do so.

"Why do you want this man?"

The gunmetal eyes lifted, turned, bored into her. She thought he was not going to give her an answer but at last he said:

"I had his name, only his name. It wasn't enough. I needed to know exactly what he looked like so that, day or night, I could recognize him instantly; so there could never be any chance of a mistake." He hoped that she would not again ask him why. She did not, but she knew, just the same, he was certain of it.

★ ★ ★

73

He shook hands with both men at the busy, noisy railroad depot at Claymore, steam billowing, the atmosphere heavy with the smell of hot oil: I. D. Rogan and M. A. Rogan. They were brothers, though were not often taken as such, Irvin being tall and bulky and loud, Myron a head shorter and a lightweight and somewhat retiring by nature.

"Real glad you found the lady, son," Irvin said waving his cigar. Myron stood at his brother's side, nodding, smiling mildly. "And well, then, did you find what it was you went there to find?"

"Yes, I surely did."

"Good. That's good. Mighty attractive lady, too," said Irvin, chuckling. Myron beamed.

"She is that," the man said. The recollection of her regular features, her slim, swan neck and the marvellous honey colour of her eyes was indeed with him and he suspected it would remain so for some while.

"Glad to have been of help, son,"

said Irvin enigmatically.

"You've finished your own business in this part of the country?"

"Business is never finished, as such," Irvin said. "It's true we're now headed back to Chicago, but we'll be back again this way no doubt. Rogan Telegraph is reaching out all over, right into the smaller communities now." He gave a nudge of an elbow. Your Beauville could've done with a wire." Irvin laughed deeply and richly, exhaling blue smoke from his mouth and down his large, hairy nostrils.

"It's not my Beauville."

"Come visit us," murmured Myron, "should you come to Chicago."

"I thank you kindly." He shook hands with them again and departed along the platform.

A woman in an elegant travelling cape and, for Claymore, a most fashionable hat, joined the Rogan brothers.

"Ah, there you are at last, Abigail."

"Who was that, Irvin? That man?"

She peered after the big man who was just then disappearing through billowing steam.

"A friend from some years ago," said Irvin, "whom we met again by chance and were able to assist in a small way; or perhaps in more than a small way, at that. Take a good look while you can, my dear; then when you get back to Chicago you can tell all of your friends that you saw Frank Ambler."

5

THE train that the Rogans had taken would have been of no use to him; he had to strike out in another direction, to join up with another railroad.

Two other passengers were on the stage, a drummer in a tight suit and a fawn derby who reeked of whiskey and who dozed sweatily during the entire, jolting journey to the town of Barrow, and a woman in her early thirties, slim and a touch over average height, who was dressed tastefully in a dark blue dress and a light grey travelling cloak and a blue tricorn hat trimmed with pale grey fur, clothing which was impeccably neat and clean, yet which bore the suggestion of frequent wear. Her face was heart shaped, her hair dark, and though her clear skin was a little pale, her lips were full and her eyes reminded him at once of the other woman's eyes, but were of a richer, darker honey. Throughout the journey, though she gave Ambler the faintest of polite smiles when he settled in opposite her, showed no indication whatsoever to engage him in conversation. When she was not staring almost dreamily at the infinite countryside as it went drifting by, she was sitting with her head tilted back slightly and her eyes lightly closed. Ambler simply let her be, sensing she might be thankful for that. Seeing her, glimpsing her eyes in particular, however, had carried his own thoughts back to Emily Chater; and he had more to draw upon from those visits than otherwise might have been the case upon such short acquaintance. Certainly, it was true that it had been the names of Irvin and Myron Rogan that had so readily opened her door to him yet by the time he had finally taken his leave of her it seemed to him — and perhaps it had been partly because of the task they had settled down to together, sorting through her late father's photographs — that there had grown between them an easy rapport. It fell well short of any kind of social intimacy yet was something that was beyond ordinary courtesy. As he had left her house for the last time she had come out onto the porch with him and they had clasped hands as older friends might have done. In his mind her touch had seemed to linger for an instant longer than might have been considered usual or even proper; and before he turned away she had said: "Take care."

Take care. He had to smile as the Claymore-Beauville-Barrow stage, Beauville now well behind it, went lurching onward, overly warm inside, musty, what air there was, fouled with the sour whiskey-smell from the drummer's open, snoring mouth. It was not a journey that Ambler felt he would care to repeat.

Wherever Frank Ambler went he nearly always drew a few curious glances, and the railroad depot at Barrow was no exception. The clerk gave him covert scrutiny when Ambler bought his ticket to Kellerman, as did the florid-faced porter; and among a group of rowdy men who obviously had passed their time waiting for the train in one of Barrow's several saloons, a neatly attired man whose profession could scarcely have been made more plain had he had an ace of spades pinned to a lapel, had regarded Ambler several times with a most singular expression that seemed to be partly curiosity and partly dislike. Ambler, having no desire to draw upon himself more close attention than necessary, and certainly no wish to get involved in some argument with a stranger who seemed well on his way to becoming drunk, contrived to direct his interest elsewhere; yet he could not quite remain unmindful of the snide presence of the man even after Ambler himself had turned half away. Also among the people standing at the depot was the uncommunicative woman who had been on the stage right through to Barrow, but she was some little distance away, near to her quite small amount of baggage, and did not appear to be at all aware of Ambler's presence; or if she was aware of it, evinced no particular interest in him. Ambler himself, though taking care not to arouse undue interest among others, did take stock of everyone who passed back and forth along the platform. While he did not seriously expect to encounter Ford here, and though the man's likeness, from the Chater photograph, was firmly established in his mind, Porter's caution was also still fresh in his memory. Whatever some folk might contend, Ford was not without friends all through this stretch of country.

Ambler's attention came unobtrusively

back to the thin man in the trim grey suit and his three companions. Now they all seemed to be searching through their various pockets, presumably looking for their train tickets, and they had therefore, at least for the present time, no further interest in the tall, powerful-looking man waiting quietly by himself at the far end of the platform. Yet Ambler could not help conjecturing that one or all of this group, even adversely affected by liquor as they appeared to be, might have a more sinister purpose in boarding this train. Perhaps they had in fact been waiting in Barrow until such time as he should put in an appearance; for he had no doubt whatsoever that by this time the word was well and truly out all through the territory: "Frank Ambler's on his way south, looking for Ford." Ambler was wearing the citified clothes he had had on when he had been in Beauville and, as had been the case there, no gun.

When the noisy, steaming locomotive

with its two passenger cars, two freight cars and yellow caboose came rolling at last into Barrow, Ambler lost no time in boarding it.

Now, leaning back in his seat, eyes narrowed but remaining mentally alert, he wondered if leaving the pistol in the leather bag that he had stowed in the rack above his head had been altogether a wise thing to do. He thought the matter over but decided that he would allow the gun to remain where it was until he reached Kellerman; to get out of his seat now and lift the bag down might well draw to him unwanted attention. Still, the thought itself had been a salutary warning to him, for every turn of the clattering wheels beneath him was taking him deeper into the regions of which he had little personal knowledge, and in which Ford was apparently accustomed to moving. What was the name that had been given him? The Death Man. Ambler might once have smiled over it, yet thinking of it now brought back with a clutch of his belly, the reality, the finality of death, of Bob's death, manacled, at the hands of a bounty hunter. So now, thought Ambler, here he was returning to the habits of a time which he believed he would never know again, there to relive a sombre season of the past. No-one else on the face of the earth could have beckoned him back there but Robert Ambler, though that young man could not be rediscovered in those regions, only the fond recollections of him, smiling and headstrong. Bob Ambler, dead. Recurring in his mind, drumming at his consciousness, was the same question, one which would return again and again in coming days and weeks: *If I were Ford, what would I do?*

The windows were smeared, dirty, all of their surrounding woodwork gritty, and the throat-filling smell of steam and smoke and oil permeated the old, sun-dried car as it went hammering along, nodding to its own insistent rhythm. The large, worn, green-covered seats seemed to diminish even the huskiest of their occupants but from the place where he sat, down near the back, Ambler could see an elderly couple, their somnolent heads nodding with the unceasing motion of the train, and beyond them, the pale, pretty woman from the stage, sitting alone. At the top end of the car was the tipsy man in the tailored grey suit, white shirt and black string tie and his three loud, laughing companions. This group, upon arriving in the car had reversed two seats and were sitting two-facing-two, small suitcases stacked to make a table upon which bright playing cards slipped and flickered and were flipped over. The players were also passing a bottle around and from time to time a joyous shout would go up and the greenbacks would be gathered in and more whiskey would be swigged; and then the dealing would resume. The man in the grey suit seemed to have lost interest in Ambler.

Ambler still kept a wary eye on all

of the card players but also thought about the town of Kellerman which he should reach maybe an hour after sundown. Several places had come to him by word of mouth that linked them, even though tenuously, to Ford; but the name of this particular place had cropped up on more than one occasion. 'Why Kellerman?' he thought. True, it was said to be a larger place than Barrow, certainly bigger than Beauville, a thriving, busy town no doubt, brief host to countless itinerants, the centre for a half-dozen ranches and a number of homesteads, and he had become aware that it was the nearest town of any kind to the Kellerman Silver Mine from which it took its name, and which was situated up in the rugged, scarred foothills of the Schaeffer Range. But none of these circumstances should have drawn particular attention from Ford. In Ambler's opinion there was but one thing that would fetch the bounty hunter to any particular area more than once and that was the possibility of substantial gain. Perhaps Ford had by this time discovered the true identities of the men who had taken the Beauville bank, and in spite of what must be the now certain knowledge that Frank Ambler was looking for him and all that such a thing implied, had been pulled back to that town by this irresistible magnetism, the prospect of money. And whether the man was in Kellerman or not, Ambler had become convinced that Ford would be somewhere in that stretch of country down there and that sooner or later, for any number of reasons, he would have to show. Now, as the train went swaying onwards, its leaping shadow with long smoke streaming, cast across the cuttings and rock pinnacles that went sliding by, Ambler permitted himself a brief time of ease, watching the changing countryside, the heat-haze across the distant hills, patches of almost green grass, places of dry clay and stunted brush and tumbleweeds. Across one of the flats more generously grassed than some of the others, a few drifting, reddish cattle grazed and for a few minutes, several cowboys on wild-eyed ponies came racing alongside the train, whooping soundlessly under the noise of it, waving their big hats, only to go wheeling away to vanish again into rising dust.

When he came to himself he first sensed, then saw, that something was wrong. Three of the car players, no doubt affected by the heat and by the whiskey they had drunk, had slumped back in their seats, heads lolling; but the man in grey, the one who seemed to have favoured Ambler with such baleful scrutiny at the Barrow depot, had got up out of his place and was now standing swaying, in the aisle, and with one hand braced on the back of a seat, was leaning over the pale woman who, by all indications, turning her head away to look out of the window, found his presence unwelcome. As, with a lurch of the car, he staggered and all but fell across her, Ambler saw one of her slim arms come up instinctively as though to shield herself. Ambler rose from his own seat and made his way deliberately up the swaying car. He had almost reached them by the time the gambler saw him, and half turned. But Ambler was quick and had the advantage of not being half drunk, so it was to be no contest. Grasping the man by the front of his shirt, bunching it in his big fist, he jerked him upright and pulled him close.

"Let that hand go inside your coat, friend," said Ambler softly, "and you won't deal off another deck inside two months." The erstwhile card players were coming back to a confused reality. "Don't turn your head," Ambler continued, 'but let your partners know that if they start anything, you're the one who's going to have the first problem." The gambler, sweat beaded on his narrow, pale face, called:

"Don't move, boys!" The three, one

of whom had been half out of his seat, subsided.

"Well done," said Ambler, low and hard. Suddenly he straightened his arm, let go of the man's shirt so that he was flung away and staggered backwards, and even against the counter-pull of the moving train, slammed hard against the narrow end door of the car. With disconcerting speed for such a big man, Ambler followed up. "Get back in your seat. Don't get out of it again this side of Kellerman. And from here to there, don't even turn your head."

The man favoured Ambler with a look of unalloyed malevolence but did as he was bid, and the foursome that had been so filled with ebullient spirits a little time before now fell broodingly quiet. Ambler had turned to go back down the car to resume his own seat but became aware that the woman's slim, gloved hand was partly raised, so he paused, and at her indication, sat down at her side.

"Thank you," she said. "I'm afraid

90

I'd become a little alarmed."

"With good reason," said Ambler. "But I doubt you'll have any more trouble. How far are you travelling?"

"Just to Kellerman, Mr . . . "

"Ambler. Frank Ambler. I'm going to Kellerman too, as it happens. If you wish, I'll see you right to wherever it is you have to go."

"That is most thoughtful of you, Mr Ambler. My name is Freda Shearman. Normally I'd not be travelling alone, but my husband has been working at the Kellerman Mine for several months, building up our funds, so now I'm going to Kellerman to join him. We hope to buy some land or perhaps a small business somewhere out here." Her voice was smooth and low-pitched and as she had been looking at him he had been reminded once again of Emily Chater; the look in the eyes it was, nothing more, for this older woman beside him, though certainly attractive enough, was somewhat colourless when compared

91

with his recollections of Emily, lacking the other woman's spontaneous warmth and vibrancy and ready smile. Indeed, this woman on the train, for someone who, by the minute, was coming closer to a husband from whom she had been separated for some while, seemed oddly dispirited. Perhaps though, he thought, this was merely the result of a long and uncomfortable journey by stage and in only marginally greater comfort by train, in oppressive heat; and the unwanted attentions of the gambling man would surely not have improved her peace of mind.

When the train pulled grindingly into Kellerman and stood, steam billowing, at the depot there, Ambler saw to it that Freda Shearman was able to depart quietly from it without any further embarrassment and that her few pieces of baggage, along with his own, were taken right away to the nearest hotel, the Alhambra. At the desk in the lobby he raised his hat to her as the porter prepared to show the woman to her room. For the second time in the past two hours, she said:

"Thank you Mr Ambler, I am most indebted to you."

She seemed to make one last intent study of his face before turning away and following the porter up the stairs.

When Ambler himself was established in his room, having first had a bath drawn, he had changed out of his more formal and eastern-looking travelling attire into levis, blue denim shirt and black, shallow-crowned, wide-brimmed hat; he had also buckled on shellbelt and holster with its heavy, well-oiled long pistol. The clothing was clean but plainly had seen long service and it was being worn with what was apparently greater ease and familiarity than had the suit he had put aside.

He wanted to lose no time in seeking out the local law in Kellerman, which he viewed as his likeliest early link with Ford.

6

CORDRY straightened up off the edge of the desk and he, too, grasped hands briefly with Ambler. Perhaps touching thirty, Cordry had a narrow, bony face with small, dark eyes. His cord pants were tucked into the tops of his cowman's boots and over a green and black checkered shirt he wore a soft leather vest; his hair was sandy and bunched over his collar at the back. The sleeves of his shirt were rolled halfway up forearms which were lightly haired and densely freckled. He did not say a great deal but when he did speak his voice had a stick-snapping brittleness about it that seemed to match his bony frame and sharp features.

Altogether different in appearance and manner was Ferron, big, with a thick body and swede-head set on a short neck, he had a shine of sweat on his forehead and upper lip, and his pale grey shirt showed discs of sweat under the arms. Ferron seemed often to be engaged in looking around the office for items which he was failing to find, so that there was a good deal of moving back and forth, opening doors and drawers and slamming them all shut again.

"There's only the two of us here, Ambler, an' it's a sizeable an' busy place, Kellerman." Ferron's voice was of lighter weight than might have been expected in such a bulky individual, and with a suggestion of chesty hoarseness about it. "If it ain't payday at one o' the cattle outfits hereabouts, then it is at the damn' mine, an' them boys want to hoorah somewhat, when they do come in."

"Good for business," Ambler murmured.

"Yeah. Yeah, I guess," said Ferron looking about and then patting each of his pockets in turn. Abruptly then he stood quite still and his pouched eyes centred on Ambler. "Listen, Ford come here about eighteen month back. Brung in a feller called Stowell. Asa Stowell."

"Dead?" asked Ambler mildly.

"Stiff as a board," crackled Cordry. "In a wagon."

Ferron pulled out a drawer of his desk, looked somewhat despondently at its contents, closed it again, glancing up at Ambler.

"Yuh carryin' any kind o' warrant?"

"No."

"No paper? Nothin'?"

"No. I'm on my own, acting strictly on my own. What I do have is admissions of certain mistakes that were made that can't be unmade. First I had word from the Beauville sheriff — and I've talked with him since — that a man had been fetched in dead; then that it was the wrong man."

"We heard about that," Cordry said. "Been all up an' down the country, that has."

96

"Then I won't need to waste any more breath on it," said Ambler, glancing at him.

"An' I won't, neither," Ferron said. "I told yuh, Ford was here about a year an' a half back, an' since then we ain't seen a whisker o' the man." Ferron was wheezing ever so slightly as he talked. "Now what that means to yuh an' whatever yuh figure to do, let me say this, Ambler, an' I bear in mind your good cause an' who yuh are, an' so on; I got enough on my plate here as marshal in this damn' town without lookin' for more. I got to say that, right out. An' half o' the time I don't know whether I'm winnin' or losin'. An' I'll say this plain, too; I don't in partic'lar need no goddamn' shootin' problems in Kellerman on top o' them that allers comes up anyway, one time an' another. In fact, I flat out don't aim to have none. Now if yuh're dead set on runnin' down Ezra Ford there ain't a lot I can do to stop yuh even if I'd a mind to. But I'll tell yuh this,

Ambler, I don't want a thing like that blowin' up right here in Kellerman. I shore don't want that."

"No more do I," Ambler told him, "but in the finish that might not be all my choice. If it does come out to be my choice, if I can pick the ground, I won't take Ezra Ford on your streets, Ferron. Nonetheless I have to say that what you've told me and what I've heard elsewhere doesn't exactly square."

"What the hell's that supposed to mean?" Cordry demanded in his crackling voice.

Ambler turned his head. "It means," he said, "that I came here to Kellerman and didn't go to some other place because the word was that Ford had been here more than once in more recent times. That is to say, in recent weeks." He turned his attention back to Ferron. "I repeat, that's why I'm here."

"What yuh heard at a distance ain't my problem," Ferron said, wheezing.

"I know that," Ambler nodded. "It

could have been said to draw me well away from where Ford really is, give him more time to move on, if he plans to move on. But somehow I don't believe that's the case. Be sure of this," and he let his eyes move deliberately to Cordry and back to Ferron, "I intend to find out if he is here, or nearby, or has been, or not, before *I* move on." There followed a silence that ran on longer than usual.

"Just so yuh keep it peaceable while yuh're doin' the lookin'," said Ferron. Having said what he had said he appeared not to want to give ground, at least not while Cordry was there.

"I'll have my eye on yuh," Cordry said to Ambler.

Ambler ignored him but said to Ferron:

"On the train through from Barrow there was a card doctor along with two or three other loudmouths who'd been too long at the bottle, and he turned out not to have good enough manners. One thing led to another and we had words about it. Thin man in a grey suit, skin the colour of old milk. A dresser. Who would that be?"

"Sounds like Ed Massey for sure, runs a saloon, the Silver Deck. Ed's been out o' town a few days."

"Well, he's back," Ambler said.

"Ed Massey's kind of a good man to avoid," Ferron said. "He's got one or two real hard-noses down there in that place o' his. Will Eckhardt is one that it pays to steer clear of."

"What does Eckhardt look like?"

Ferron pursed his full lips.

"Big red-headed bastard with a flat nose. Hands like shovels."

"Then he wasn't among the ones on the train."

"Aw, yuh'd have knowed about it real soon if he had been," Cordry commented in a way that Ambler considered was not too far short of relish. "He's a real mean hombre. Will is. I seen Will pick up a thirteen-stone miner an' *throw* the bastard."

"If yuh've run afoul o' Massey

already," said Ferron, looking serious, "yuh'd be well advised to not show your face in the Silver Deck."

"I'll bear that advice in mind," said Ambler agreeably. "I don't have any further interest in Massey unless of course he should turn out to be connected with Ford in some way."

"Why would yuh think that?" Cordry asked.

"I don't, necessarily," said Ambler, "but I've learned in my time to rule nothing out until it can be eliminated as a probability."

Cordry, his Adam's apple active, hooked thumbs in his belt.

"That Ford," he said, "he's a weird bastard. He any kin to the Ford that shot Jesse James?"

"Not that I know of," Ambler said. It was not the first time he had been asked that question.

"Ambler," Ferron said, perhaps, on reflection, thinking that he had appeared to be a mite unsympathetic earlier, "that was a hell of a thing that happened to the boy. Not right for a young 'un to come to it, just like that. Unfair."

"The world offers none of us any contract to be fair," said Ambler. "Mistakes are made, sometimes real bad ones, so that all that can be done, after, is to overlook them or square for them. Ford didn't have to kill him, of that I'm certain."

"He's said to be right well heeled, this Ford," Cordry remarked, "though not so's folks would notice to look at him."

"He ought to have something put by," said Ambler. "In some quarters the best reckoning of the bounty he's picked up just over the past six years is close enough to forty thousand."

Ferron's mouth hung open. Cordry did not raise his eyebrows but whistled softly. They both fell quiet. Ambler thought they were possibly calculating how many full years of a local lawman's pay such a sum would represent. Ambler believed, too, that they might be thinking, as he was, that a man such as Ford could buy a lot of silence and even a few very good quality lies for a fraction of that kind of money.

At that point Cordry nodded, crossed and picked his hat off a peg and wandered out of the office. He paused a moment on the boardwalk then hitched at his belt and strolled away. When the door had opened there had come to them the distant, tinny music from saloons and the sounds of people laughing. There was plenty of movement up and down Main.

"Busy night," Ambler observed.

"This is quiet," said Ferron. "There's not a lot o' riders in town an' nobody at all from the silver mine, right now."

"The Beauville bank pair," said Ambler. "Any word? Any talk?"

Ferron shook his head slowly.

"Not around these parts; but we git new faces through here all the time. They could be here now an' we'd never know. They could be five hundred mile away. They could be in Mexico by now, which wouldn't be such a bad idea if Ford's dead set on runnin' 'em down."

"I doubt that Ford will concern himself," said Ambler, "until it's known, or near sure, who they are."

Ferron nodded, acknowledging what he saw as the logic of that. He began to paw about on his littered desk, looking for something else he could not find, and Ambler read it as a hint, and departed. But after he had gone out, Ferron's vagueness evaporated and he crossed at once to the doorway and watched the tall man walking away until he could no longer distinguish him among others in the spills of lamplight across the boardwalks.

Ambler crossed Main and made his way back to the hotel and was reaching out for the door when a shot was fired at him. By all reasonable calculations the bullet ought to have hit him. That it did not, he thought afterwards, might well have been because whoever it was shooting was anxious to get it done and get away. Perhaps indeed getting away had become the dominant thought in the mind of the shooter and that had led to his poor judgement and to Ambler's good luck. As it was, the slug flicked the back of his shirt before banging into the woodwork of the hotel; then Ambler was down on all-fours. Several people on the street had scattered when the shot came, a woman or child screamed and at least one citizen, seeing the big fellow at the hotel doorway go down, thought that he had been hit, and a shout went up:

"There's a man shot!"

Ambler, on one knee now, had his eyes firmly on the mouth of an alley across the street, trying to decide if that had been where the shooter had stood. If so, it was empty now. Two passers-by came hesitantly to him.

"It's all right," he said.

Somewhat circumspectly the night clerk came out of the Alhambra. Cordry, the deputy marshal, appeared from somewhere, jogging, waving his arms at people who were beginning to gather.

"Git on away! Don't bunch up!" That sure dispersed them for, carrying as it did the suggestion of further shooting. Cordry also surveyed the opposite side of the street. "Yuh git a look at who it was?"

"No," said Ambler, rising.

"I'll go check the back lots across there," Cordry said, looking first at where the bullet had struck the front of the Alhambra. Ambler told him that it could well be a wasted effort. His own attention had shifted to the upstairs windows, some open, some darkened, of the various establishments across the street from where they stood. One of them was the Silver Deck. Before Cordry crossed the street to do, anyway, what he had said he intended to do, he gave Ambler a quite bleak look. "Didn't take long for the fat to git in the fire once yuh got here." Ambler made no reply, but now here was Ferron as well, sweating profusely, asking Cordry where he was sloping off to. "It was him that somebody took the shot at," Cordry said, nodding towards Ambler. "I'm goin' to have a look around."

"Christ," said Ferron. "Go on then." To Ambler he said: "So it's started already."

"Your man's just been all through that one. Listen, Ferron, I'm real sorry to hear that you've got all this work, but some bastard tried to *nail* me. I don't really much care whether it was in Kellerman, Tombstone, Denver or Dodge, I take exception to it, and if you or that skinny feller who was just here can't get to know who did it, then I'll set about finding out myself even if I have to kick some doors in, and I want you to hear and understand that."

"Don't git on your high horse," Ferron wheezed. "We'll do the best we can, like we allers do, but I knowed as soon as yuh showed up here it was all gonna tear at the seams."

When Ambler left him and went on inside the Alhambra, the night clerk who had preceded him had not gone in behind his desk but was still standing in the lobby as though he was no longer sure of what to do. He moistened his lips, his eyes gone large as the big man came in.

"You plannin' to stay long in Kellerman, Mr Ambler?"

"As long as it takes," said Ambler.

7

IN his room Ambler sat on the edge of the cot, his mind filled with the events of past days, the disbelief; the shock, the heavy weight of grief, the impotent fury of those first hours, trying to grapple with all that, then finally heading for Beauville. And by the time he had reached that place his fury had resolved itself into a cold purpose, to find Ford himself and to get the straight of it, then if necessary, deal with it.

If Porter had been expecting the rampaging Frank Ambler he had so graphically predicted for Makin's benefit, then such a man had not materialized in his office. The one who had come had been that much more alarming for being quiet, but with an air of utter resolve about him.

For Ambler himself his talk with

Porter came back to him now, all of it, not simply what he had told the marshal and the deputy here in Kellerman.

"Ford won't just let it happen," Porter said.

Ambler walked to the window, thumbs hooked in his belt, stood staring out. Porter sat down in the chair behind his desk, opened a drawer and fumbled around for a stogie and matches. When he had lit up, blowing sweet-smelling smoke above his head, he went on: "Don't be misled about Ford. People often give out that because o' what the man is, he's got no friends at all. Now, whether or not you an' me would think of 'em as friends is another matter altogether. Sure, some o' them that Ford has might be such as don't want to wind up on the wrong side o' the man. He's damn' dangerous, is Ford." He did not know whether or not the man at the window was taking due heed of him. "Ambler, there's somethin' I have to tell yuh,

110

an' no way do I want to do it, an' there's no easy way to do it." He did get Ambler's full attention then, though perhaps more because of what was in his tone rather than what he had said. Ambler turned his head to look at Porter. "After we'd been over to talk with Makin an' after he went an' got a-hold of the bounty money, Ford left Beauville, went the same night." Porter drew on his stogie, exhaled a stream of smoke. "I come on back to where the boy . . . to where your brother was, an' I took another good look at him. Whether or not I shoulda done it afore I won't argue, but Ambler, I got to say there was these marks on his wrists."

"Marks?"

Porter nodded, shifted slightly in his chair. Ambler straightened, turned fully to face Porter, allowed his hands to fall to his sides, standing immobile then, concentrating fully on the man sitting behind the desk.

"I'd say the boy had been wearin'

manacles. At some stage he'd been wearin' manacles."

After what seemed a long silence Ambler said softly:

"At some stage."

Porter now glanced at the stogie with apparent distaste before stubbing it out in a shallow brass bowl on the desk; then he looked up at Ambler.

"We'll never know." He realized as soon as he had said it that it made no kind of sense. Indeed, Ambler responded at once.

"He wouldn't have put irons on him *after* he was shot. You say they definitely weren't on when you helped carry him in?"

Porter shook his head, his glance dropping away. Then he said that if they had been he would have at once resisted paying Ford anything, and he knew that Makin would have been pleased to have had that point to argue about. Ambler made no further comment on it but Porter knew that if it were possible to say that Ford's own death warrant had been signed at a particular instant in time, then he recognized that it had just been done. Ambler, in appearance, had surprised the Beauville peace officer; plainly a man of the open range, hard, powerfully built and with a disturbing fixity of eye yet deceptively low-pitched voice, he had arrived on the mid-afternoon stage wearing clothes that in other circumstances would have marked him as some kind of buyer or surveyor from the east. After putting up at the Lonsdale Hotel however, he had emerged in levis, pale blue denim shirt and shallow, wide-brimmed black hat; his boots were high-heeled, well made but also scuff-worn, and the wide, dark leather belt at his middle with its unremarkable brass buckle had obviously seen much service. Surprisingly, he wore no firearm. His name had gone before him, though that was nothing new, and he had drawn much discreet but curious scrutiny both as he had walked from the stage depot to the Lonsdale and later from there to the Beauville jail. So this was Frank Ambler. The most lingering of the looks following the tall, easy-striding man were those of women, much of it covert, from under lashes.

Porter drew a breath and said:

"Yuh got any notion yourself o' where he mighta gone?"

"Somewhere down along the Cheyne River. Kellerman maybe."

"Yuh heard somethin' then?"

"I've heard a great many things, Porter, some of them conflicting."

"Ford will have heard as many of you, I reckon."

"I've made no secret of where I am or what I'm doing. It's best not to have any illusions. He would always know I'd be coming for him."

"How do yuh plan on gettin' to Kellerman? Ride from here? It's a good long piece."

"No, I'll take the stage on down

to Barrow. The railroad goes through there and through Kellerman."

He had scarcely mentioned the part of the Beauville law and the town's bank in the matter of sending out the wrong name but Porter himself had raised the matter of the witnesses, since he thought, come what may, he might just as well get everything out on the table, face up.

"They've gone. I don't know where to. They lit out when they heard you was comm' here."

"I'm not concerned with them any more. They've got to live with themselves, not me. If Bob was manacled, Ford had got the drop. In the end it's all down to Ford."

Porter rose as Ambler prepared to leave.

"Remember what I said: Ford's got people who'd help him; mebbe more than that."

Ambler nodded and walked out.

Now, in Kellerman, it was late evening and he had been told by men

whose word ought to be trustworthy
that Ford had not been here in a long
time; and he could almost hear again
the gunshot that had all but blown him
down.

8

THE names were out, the ones from the Beauville bank. Porter said afterwards — for after all that it was he who tumbled to them — that a man ought to have been kicked from here to at the very least northern Montana for not seeing it earlier. He had been engaged in bundling up some old reward dodgers prior to burning them when he had noticed one in particular with two faces on it and relating to a freight depot robbery in Bitter Falls some long time back. As soon as he saw the very good likeness of Orv Lowry he knew that he had his 'Bob Ambler'. Alongside Lowry was a quite ugly man called Jim Gemmel and when Porter said the names over to himself aloud and stared again at the artist's likeness in particular of Lowry, he was utterly convinced that he was looking at the accomplices of the late, unresponsive, Joe Half. So certain in fact was Porter that he took the old dodger across to Makin at the bank and at the same time arranged for a man to ride to the Fremont telegraph.

"No doubt about it this time," Porter said, his face flushed and his eyes bright. Even Makin, a naturally cautious man who had been made even more cautious through recollections of past and public errors, felt bound to agree.

"The likeness is certainly astonishing."

The Bitter Falls reward for this pair was $1,000.

"One way an' another they're startin' to be worth a lot o' dinero," Porter said. "It's goin' up by the minute."

"We ought to have made our reward conditional upon recovering at least three-quarters of this bank's money," mused Makin. It had all been done in such a lather at the time, that had been the trouble, and it was, if nothing else, a salutary lesson in the undesirability of haste, especially in matters of finance.

* * *

It was a rundown place on the far side of the Cheyne River and the closest civilization, if you could call it that, was Kellerman. Zachary Eder ran a few scrawny stock at Baker's Creek, hunted a little, and during real thin times had been known to hire on at the Kellerman Mine; but his lack of hearing made that an unattractive not to say dangerous proposition since, unless he actually saw it, he never did know when one of the heavy ore wagons might be approaching.

So here they were in their light-stepping excitement and their bulging canvas sack, Eder's kinsman, Gemmel, and his younger accomplice, Lowry, Gemmel making reassuring mimes to Eder about not having been followed, and then developing other, even more appealing, semaphores which Eder

119

interpreted as the promise of generous recompense in return for his sanctuary.

They had to do something with the sack, of course, and in the finish, after a good deal of confused waving of arms and silently-mouthed argument, there had been nothing else for it but to put it underneath the house and nail the floorboards down again and drag the furniture back. So with that the second phase of the robbery at the bank at Beauville came to an end.

* * *

Ford was as one with the deepest shadows, standing only three feet away so that they could speak in voices that were scarcely audible. They were concerned that even small sounds were inclined to carry, at night. The place was a lean-to structure on one end of a large barn standing on the eastern fringe of Kellerman, a place which had a seldom-used corral alongside it and with a huddle of other darkened, even more nondescript structures nearby. Ford had been there first, and had waited with characteristic patience.

"You took good care, comin' here?"

"Of course. Yes."

"So then, is there any new word?"

"First, Frank Ambler is here." There was the faintest rustle of movement as Ford drew even closer, bringing his earthy smell with him. "He's at the Alhambra; but he's hired himself a horse and taken to riding out every day."

"Riding out where?"

"I don't know. Just looking around. Asking questions." The speaker could have no idea of the effect, if any, this information might have had on Ford. Presently:

"What else? Anything?"

"Oh yes indeed. Word by telegraph. The Beauville boys. Names."

"Ah!" It was emphatic, but little more than a breath. "Who?"

"Orv Lowry, Jim Gemmel."

After a pause:

"Lowry. Of course." A question was hanging in the darkness, so Ford added: "He could easily have been taken for Bob Ambler. Same height, weight, colour."

"Frank Ambler is . . . "

"Is what?"

"Very dangerous."

"He'll move on. When he finds nothing here. All wild animals do it. No food to be had in one place, so finally they move on to another." Whether or not his opinion was accepted was unclear for it drew no response.

"He very nearly got moved on in a box the same night he got here."

"Yet he's still alive. Looking around, you said, asking questions. Nearly means very little. Very little."

"There's a lot could be said to that. Let's leave it for now."

Ford apparently agreed for he now returned to the other matter.

"Lowry and Gemmel."

"Across the border maybe, by this time?"

"I think not."

"Where then?"

"Obviously I can't be sure; but maybe not as far from here as we might think. It confirms a line of thought I've had all along, but with not much to back it. I did have a vague word, not much more than opinion. It's not that easy to sift out what's of value; but I've been reluctant to leave this place, an' it does seem to me now that it's paid off."

"So they're holed-up somewhere around here?"

"Maybe holed-up. It opens up a new line o' thought, you can say that."

"Do you think they'll still have the money with them?"

"Yeah. Oh yes. They'd not be likely to stash that any place that they weren't able at least to watch. Near to fifteen thousand remember. That, and their bounty comes to near seventeen. Could be more out; I've got a faint notion of earlier matters. Anyway, seventeen. For that I'll risk Frank Ambler." Ford sounded more certain of himself than ever now. Allowing his thoughts to settle, in particular on Gemmel, he had recalled something. Something of value.

9

WHEN more brush was thrown on and the fire blazed up, Ambler was there. They had heard no horse. He must have come just so far, picketed the animal, then come in some way on foot. To range-bred men it was both surprising and not a little alarming. When the man who had fed the fire made to step towards him, Ambler held one hand up. He had now had enough of taking things at face value and wanted to assert authority right from the start.

"Wait."

Around the corner of the chuck wagon the cook came suddenly into view. Ambler's right shoulder dipped, there was a quick glitter at his side and the firelight was flickering on a long pistol. In the breath-holding stillness they heard the sharp sound of it being cocked.

"Come on right out, cookie," Ambler said. "Come to the fire."

The man wasted no time at all doing as he was bid, hunch-shouldered, bald, a fringe of ginger whiskers. The first man was still standing, the three others sat at the fire, two holding tin mugs.

"What crew is this?"

"Fetterman's. Lazy F."

"Just take it easy then, boys, and listen. I've got no business with Lazy F one way or another, and certainly no quarrel. An hour ago I crossed a loop of the Cheyne River. I need to know if a man came through here, a tall man with a black moustache and wearing dark clothes; or maybe if you heard a rider but didn't see who it was."

A silence ran on after he had finished speaking and as he looked from face to face he knew that they, simple range riders, were wary of him, the way he had spoken, the no-nonsense confidence that rang in his voice. But finally one of them, the narrow, sinewy man who had stepped forward at the outset and whom Ambler thought was perhaps the tophand in this crew, said:

"Nobody come here, mister. Nobody. If anybody had come he woulda been on Fetterman land just like you are now, either to stay or to move right on at our say-so."

"I'll move on," said Ambler, "in my own good time."

"Are yuh a marshal or what?"

"Or what."

"Listen mister, yuh better talk up real good. Whoever or whatever yuh are don't change the fact that this here ain't open range, an' Fetterman, he don't take at all kindly to folks jes' driftin' through, around his beef, unless they got business with him, personal. Fetterman's had a peck o' trouble in the past, an' he ain't above dealin' hard with them as cain't give good reasons fer bein' on his land." Clearly, drawn gun or not, this man was not about to be faced down in front of his own crew, and Ambler had to give him unspoken credit for that. He saw that some face-saving would not be out of the way.

"Ease off, mister. There's no offence intended. I maybe spoke a mite hasty. It's just that I happen to be somewhat anxious to come up with this particular man for personal reasons that won't keep." He slid his heavy pistol back into its holster and the cowboy who had stood up to him must have considered that his honour was unblemished.

"Who is this feller yuh want? Could be that we'd know him by name if he's from 'round these parts."

"That wouldn't surprise me," said Ambler. "He's Ezra Ford."

All this while the range cook had been holding a tin cup and he now dropped it and it bounced off his boot but he did not trouble to retrieve it.

"Jesus. Him. The Death Man."

"Maybe so," said Ambler. "I've heard that name. Well, I'm The Retribution Man."

The tophand shook his head. "We still ain't seen nothin' o' this Ford, mister. Did hear he was around Kellerman some while back. But he ain't what yuh'd call a local man."

"By Gawd," the cook said then. "I reckon yuh must be Frank Ambler."

"I'm Frank Ambler." The tophand now rubbed his hands slowly on the front of his shirt as though they might have begun to sweat, and he was perhaps remembering how tetchy he had lately been with this man. "If by chance you should see Ford, tell him I'm coming for him."

Ambler felt that there was nothing to be gained by prolonging his visit, and left them. He had now covered a wide sweep of country out of Kellerman by means of carefully thought out forays, and although he had found no trace of Ford and had received no admission from anyone that the man had been seen recently, there was no doubt in his mind that his very presence, provided he was right in his belief that the bounty hunter was still in the vicinity, would in itself have an effect. Ambler reasoned that, for one thing, some of those he had spoken to had lied to him, and therefore Ford was quite likely to be kept fully aware of Ambler's movements; and for another, if Ford indeed was still here, the pair from Beauville must also have gone to ground in this part of the country, and might attempt to shake Ford off by using Ambler's presence to distract him. Riding on through the night towards the speckled lamps of Kellerman, Ambler thought grimly that he might yet become anybody's target. Take the gunshot on Main. Ford? Somehow he thought not. Massey? Perhaps; or one of his men. There were certain other thoughts nagging at him, or more truly, barely-formed impressions, ephemeral apprehensions which as yet he could not draw together, make any sense of; but together they added up to a growing unease that he was beset by enemies he could not see, and none of them was Ford.

By a lamp's light, after he had led

the horse into a barn at the back of the Alhambra, unsaddled it, rubbed it down, tipped feed into a trough and had seen to it that fresh water was nearby, when part way to the hotel itself he changed his mind and decided to take a look around the Silver Deck across the street, for he was still troubled about the shot that had been fired at him, and highly suspicious of Massey.

What precisely he expected to find he did not know, if indeed anything, but at least he wanted to study the front of the Alhambra from the opposite side of the street and, mindful of where the slug had struck the wall, perhaps gain a new perspective on where the shooter might have stood, whether at ground level or above. Because the hour was late, not many people were on Main. The lights in Massey's saloon were still on and there was from within an occasional burst of laughter. Ambler, however, had no intention of going inside; instead he surveyed the Alhambra from the dark mouth of the alley that ran alongside the Silver Deck. The more he thought about it the more he came to believe that this was where the shooter had stood, perhaps having seen Ambler leave the hotel, waited patiently for his return; or maybe, seeing him by chance, had yielded to the impulse of a snap shot.

The second possibility would sound like Massey or one of his cohorts. Ambler looked at the range involved and considered that the attempt had been an ambitious one. Acting on an impulse of his own he turned and walked up along the alley to the rear of the Silver Deck. Though the night was cloudy, moonless, he could distinguish several outbuildings and beyond them another, narrower street that would run parallel to Main, and upon which a few house lamps were still glowing. Directly behind the saloon itself the outbuildings formed a small yard where there were still smaller shapes that he took to be trash cans. Between the two structures farthest from him there was a gap which obviously led out to that other street; so if in fact his man had used the front alleyway for cover, his retreat need not necessarily have been into a back room of the saloon, it might have been through that passage to the back street; and once there, to anywhere else in Kellerman. Slightly disappointed to discover this other way out, was Ambler, for he had hoped that his theories might have led more positively to those at the Silver Deck. He turned and retraced his steps along the alley towards Main.

For a little time he was to wonder if he had been seen from some part of the saloon, standing in the yard, or if the encounter had been purely by chance; but whichever was the case he found himself, at the alley's corner, confronted by a hulking man half illuminated by light from the saloon, a man whose torso was thick, whose upper body was muscular and whose head was large and set upon a short, strong neck. Someone else, a smaller, slimmer figure, was behind this man whom Ambler, judging by the description that Ferron had given him, had to be Will Eckhardt; and the other would be Massey. Even as this thought was in his mind Massey stepped forward and then the two of them together formed a barrier which Ambler must pass if he wanted to continue out onto Main and so across to the hotel. Three feet short of them he stopped.

"Well now," Massey said quietly, "the second meeting."

"I'm surprised you can even remember the first one," said Ambler. Massey held the stub of a cigar between his fingers; now he dropped it to the ground and with the toe of one shoe, almost delicately extinguished it.

"So this is him," Eckhardt said in a heavy, husky voice.

"Oh yes, this is Mister Frank Ambler," Massey purred, "a man of some reputation in various parts of the

134

country, or so I do hear. A man come bent upon vengeance, so other talk tells me, for a kinsman shot to death."

Ambler stood quite still. Massey wore no visible weapon but from the train, Ambler recalled a gesture towards the inside of his coat, a move which, at the time, Ambler had advised him against completing. He would be armed, right enough, covertly, for that would be in his nature. Curiously, he could see no weapon on Eckhardt either and concluded that he was not carrying one, for he was dressed only in levis and shirt, and no hat. His hair, though it curled thickly over his ears was receding at the front, leaving the dome of his forehead with a pale, polished appearance. When Ambler looked more closely it did appear that Eckhardt was holding something in his right hand, concealed for the moment behind his leg, and for a moment Ambler was concerned that this would prove to be a Colt that he might simply have picked up on his way out of the saloon.

The very few passers-by evinced no interest at all in the small group of men standing at the mouth of the alley, for voices were not raised in a way that might have attracted attention. At one moment, Ambler thought that he glimpsed the deputy marshal, Cordry, make an appearance near the Alhambra Hotel, but if it was, he went walking away up Main without so much as a glance across the street.

"A kinsman murdered by Ezra Ford," Ambler said.

"Then a noble mission indeed," Massey observed smoothly. "However, by no means one which ought to have brought you on the prowl, in the night, onto property belonging to me." So they *had* seen him in the yard.

Ambler could hear Eckhardt's strong breathing and smell the stale stench of him, but still was not able to discern what it was that the man was holding onto.

"Not so long ago," Ambler said, "in this town, somebody took a shot at me, probably from this alley, and it wasn't such a bad shot at that; it didn't miss me by much more than a match-head. When someone does that to me I'm always anxious to know where he might have come from and where he might have bolted to, after."

"What is it you're trying to do here? Are you trying to suggest something to me, Ambler?" Massey asked, not changing his mild tone. Ambler thought that the man from the saloon was much more impressive and probably more dangerous when in control of himself, than when he was talking from drink.

"You can take what you like out of it," Ambler said. He was now quite sick of Massey, and concealed weapon or not, did not count him as a threat; but he knew that he would have to watch himself very carefully with Eckhardt.

"Then I choose to take the worst offence possible," Massey said, "for I don't cotton to being insulted when I question big mouths who think they can trespass as it suits them. Sooner or later, they have to be taught a lesson." Even as he finished speaking he was turning on his heel to mount the boardwalk and go back inside the Silver Deck.

"An' that leaves just you an' me," Eckhardt said. His right arm finally came into view and it was just as well for Ambler that he had been watchful and was already moving back and across to Eckhardt's left, for the big man's hand rose to jaw height and Ambler saw the wagon spoke that was being held with the utmost menace. Suddenly the night air hummed with it as Eckhardt whipped it around in a fast arc that, in its career, sent Ambler's hat spinning away, then banged heavily against the side wall of the saloon. Ambler ducked as the quick reverse sweep actually flicked his hair and he heard a grunt of effort burst from Eckhardt, Ambler at once weaving and retreating but never allowing his attention to stray from the shape of the advancing Eckhardt, not comfortable about his own mobility though, the pistol heavy at his side; yet he knew that if he were to draw the weapon there was a good chance that he would kill the man coming at him, or at least at this range, wound him grievously, and in spite of the menace to himself, had no wish to do either.

One thing in his favour was that Eckhardt was continuing to swing the heavy spoke in hard, flat arcs, doing his utmost to smash Ambler's head with it, while Ambler himself knew that two-handed thrusts at him with the end of the weapon, and directed at his body, would have been much more effective, infinitely more dangerous. In a series of long, deliberate paces, the one advancing, the other retreating, they had moved maybe half way along the alley, and Ambler was trying desperately to remember if anything had stood between the back corner of the saloon and the way that led out onto the back street. He had just made up his mind to take his chances, to turn and get away from the lumbering Eckhardt, when to his dismay he heard a back door flung open and the murmuring of voices in the yard, and he was also conscious of a light spilling out, perhaps from one of the back rooms, perhaps from a hand-held lamp. No doubt sent by Massey, they were about to box him in, to bar his retreat so that Eckhardt could take his time over dealing with him. Once again the big man swung the wood and the air hummed with its passage. This time however, Ambler's tactics changed abruptly, and he went in fast under Eckhardt's right arm, driving short left and right punches, and was elated when he felt the man go off balance; then Ambler was past him, turning quickly, backing now not towards the yard but towards Main. But for a large and clumsy brawler, Eckhardt, probably through sheer frustrated rage, had also turned quickly to whip the wagon spoke across in another vicious swipe and, in keeping his balance as he turned, Ambler's left arm swung wide of his body and he felt the searing impact of the blow and cried out with the pain of it. Eckhardt bellowed in triumph but hauled up short when he saw the quick glint of steel at Ambler's right side as the tall man drew.

"Far enough!" called Ambler, and there was Eckhardt framed in the glow of the lamp that was being held high by one of three men who had come around from the yard. "All hold up right there!" Ambler said clearly. His left hand was throbbing and felt as though it was afire. "Drop it," he said to Eckhardt. The ox-like man hesitated only for a moment, then did as he was bid. Out on Main most of the lamps had by now been extinguished; even those in the Silver Deck seemed either to have been turned low or doused altogether, so that the group in the alley, even though they were now nearer to Main than they had been when Ambler, backing off, had finally drawn the pistol, seemed now suspended in a velvet darkness invaded only by the yellow glow of one lamp. There was an unreal quality to the scene, the alley a place of gargoyle shadows, utter stillness for a moment, until it was breached by Eckhardt's sweating, chest-heaving movement, his pig eyes boring towards the gloom where stood the man holding the big pistol, and his shout:

"This limp bastard's bluffin'!" and came right in towards Ambler, who cocked the pistol. There seemed to be some slight responsive movement among those with the light, but Ambler had to give his whole attention to the advancing Eckhardt.

When the sharp sound of the shot came it was from somewhere out on Main. Ambler sensed but was not in a position to see the flash, but the whipping whisper of the bullet was real enough and desperately close to his right shoulder. But it was Eckhardt that it struck. The smacking sound was brutally audible and Eckhardt was punched half around, then sat down heavily, grunting. Even before Eckhardt was down Ambler had turned, but out on Main there was darkness except for the faintest of low amber lights filtering from the lobby of the Alhambra Hotel. Boots were pounding along one of the boardwalks, but obviously from someone coming along the front of the Silver Deck, and coming rapidly closer. Ambler had flattened himself against a wall, still holding the pistol, when Cordry's voice called:

"Who's that?"

"Ambler. There's a man down, shot."

The men with the lamp, seemingly unmindful of the target they would be presenting were grouped around Eckhardt who, still in a sitting position, was gasping, a good deal of blood on him, both massive hands pressed high up on his left chest near the collar bone.

Cordry, gun in hand, tilted upwards, came cautiously into the alley.

"Who is it shot?"

"Eckhardt."

"Who shot him? You?"

"No." Ambler reversed the pistol, held out by the barrel towards the deputy. "See for yourself."

"I cain't see much in this damn' light," Cordry said, "but if it ain't been fired it ain't been fired." He strode past Ambler towards the huddle around Eckhardt. "How bad is he?"

"He ain't good," somebody said. "He's losin' blood fast."

"Better git him into the Deck, then," muttered Cordry. "I'll go wake Doc Perkins, which won't be to his likin', an' see what can be done." To Ambler he said: "I'll want to know what it was all about. Where's Massey?" He inclined his head and sniffed at the pistol that was still in Ambler's hand.

"Inside, somewhere. He bowed out, left me an' Eckhardt to talk matters over." Ambler walked a few paces along the alley and picked up his hat, then came back.

"You're a bloody fool," Cordry said in his stick-snapping voice. He walked out of the alley, Ambler not far behind him. They could do what they liked with Eckhardt as far as Ambler was concerned; the man had been only a breath away from smashing Ambler's head in. He walked across Main towards the Alhambra. The sound of the shot had caused a lamp or two to come on again and several curious faces were dotted along the street. Ambler went on into the hotel. 'The second try,' he thought bitterly; for there was no doubt in his mind that the bullet that had struck Eckhardt had been intended for his own back.

10

FERRON came to the hotel early, Ambler had washed and dressed with some difficulty, for his left hand was painful and grossly swollen, and he was about to go down to breakfast when the Kellerman peace officer rapped at his door. By the looks of him, thought Ambler, he had been woken late on the previous night and told what had taken place, and his interrupted rest showed in the rawness around eyes that were now centred broodingly on Ambler.

"I want to know more about this Goddamn' nonsense with Eckhardt an' Massey."

"There's not a lot to tell," Ambler said. "I took a look around the outside of the saloon down there. Massey must have seen me and came out with his chimpanzee and they blocked my way and then he went inside again and left Eckhardt to brain me with a wagon spoke. Massey sent some more of his boys out the other way to make certain that it all took place; then somebody on Main shot at me and hit Eckhardt instead. All of which you'll have heard already from others who were there. Is Eckhardt alive?"

"What? Oh, yeah. Yeah, he ain't hurt all that bad as it happens, but he lost plenty o' blood." Ferron patted several pockets in turn, gave up and said: "What makes yuh think it was you that was shot at? It was Eckhardt stopped it. It might have been meant for Eckhardt. He's made plenty of enemies around here, Eckhardt has. Plenty."

"There was a lamp there in the alley. I think it was enough of a light to show who was who and where they were standing. I was back-on to Main, the nearest to whoever fired. It couldn't have been much closer to me. It was the second try."

Ferron stared at him pouchily.

"Yuh been trouble ever since yuh got off that train, Ambler. All this damn' business over Ford. Whole territory's buzzin' with it. Yuh brought that here to Kellerman."

"I don't think this was Ford."

"Why not? Why wouldn't it be him?"

"Ford might have missed once, but not twice. Besides, they were longish shots, both of them chances that were maybe on the down side of fifty-fifty. That's not what I've heard about Ford."

Ferron grunted non-committally. Then he said:

"What are your movements now?"

"You mean when am I leaving Kellerman?"

"Yeah, well, somethin' like that."

"When I get some believable word of Ford." Believable was there for Ferron to pick up on if he had a mind to but he did not do it. But he could not entirely suppress sarcasm.

"Word where from? Philadelphia?"

"I've got a strong feeling that Ford's

around here somewhere. The shots that were fired at me might not have been from Ford himself but they were because of me coming here for him. That's what I think."

"I don't know of no partic'lar friends of his in this town."

"People might tend not to talk about things like that," said Ambler.

"Sooner or later I git to hear of most things that go on here," Ferron said. It was not a boast. He was a lawman who had a good hold on his job in spite of all his protestations of overwork and Ambler respected that; but he said:

"Most, maybe. Not all. I'd put real money on it."

Ferron took a leisurely pace or two up the room, glanced out of the window, came back, dipped into a pocket, withdrew some coins, looked at them absently, put them back, staring at the floor. He looked up.

"Did yuh dig out the slug? The first one? The one that hit this here hotel?"

"No, but I looked at where it hit. So did your man Cordry. Why?"

"Was it from a Colt?"

"It seemed big enough. And it sounded like a Colt." And again: "Why?"

Ferron sighed, rubbing a hand all over his tired face.

"Oh, I dunno. Somethin' an' nothin'. Perkins, o' course, took the one out of Eckhardt last night. Wasn't .45. Somethin' a mite smaller. I don't mean *real* small, derringer small; but certainly not from a Colt. But it packed some punch, notwithstandin'."

Ambler thought about it. Then:

"It didn't sound like a Colt, either. Thanks for mentioning it."

"I don't know why I did," said Ferron.

He walked downstairs with Ambler but declined the invitation to breakfast. Ambler went into the dining room where there was a scattering of guests at various tables. Freda Shearman, apparently still waiting for her man, smiled and nodded to him. He responded courteously and at her gentle invitation, joined her. He got the impression she was pleased to see a friendly face.

"Your husband hasn't arrived yet, Mrs Shearman?"

"No, though I have had word from him. And I spoke to a man at a livery yesterday and I've arranged to hire out a buggy this afternoon. I'm going out to the Kellerman Mine to meet my husband and bring him back into town. We'll make our further plans after that."

"You're making the journey out to the Kellerman alone?"

"No, as it happens. I asked directions of the marshal's deputy . . . I've just forgotten his name . . .

"Cordry."

"Ah. Yes. Well, I saw him on Main yesterday and told him where I intended going. It so happens he has business out in that direction, and if I delay leaving until this afternoon, Mr Cordry will ride with me most of the way." She spoke quietly and still with a kind of wistfulness in her tone; but she turned the conversation towards Ambler himself, questioning him about his hand, for clearly he was having some trouble with it.

"One of the men from the Silver Deck Saloon," he said. "An employee of friend Massey."

"That comes right back to something you did on my behalf," she said.

"For which you had no responsibility or blame," said Ambler. Then he told her about the shot and about what had happened to Eckhardt. A small crease appeared between her brows. She told him that she could not remember hearing a shot but she had awoken to hear men shouting, and when she had looked out there had been lamps coming on along Main and movement just across the street.

"What will you do now?" Ferron had posed him the same question.

"I've still got some asking to do, some territory to cover. One thing

I do know now. The man I want, Ford, has got at least one friend here in Kellerman."

"Is it this man Massey?"

He shook his head. "I doubt that. Massey was simply looking to square what he saw as a humiliation. No, it's not Massey."

She had begun her breakfast long before he had come in and was now finished and ready to leave.

"Do please excuse me, Mr Ambler. I've a number of things that I must attend to." He rose as she got up from her chair. Turning, she paused. "If there's a doctor here in Kellerman you should have him take a look at that hand. There could be bones broken." The rich honey eyes showed concern. She went on out through the door into the lobby.

★ ★ ★

When he had ample time to think a situation through, Ford did not overlook much; and he had given Ory Lowry and Jim Gemmel a great deal of thought in preceding hours. That was what had brought him quietly to the precincts of Zachary Eder's place across a ford of the Cheyne River and along one of its sorry-looking tributaries, Baker's Creek.

The country was rough and broken, sun-parched under a brassy sky, strewn with brush, littered with stones, on one hand shimmering flats, on the other the rusty entrails of hills that eventually piled up to lie huddled against the lower shoulders of the jagged Schaeffer Range cut sharply against the sky.

How anyone could subsist in a land such as that which lay before him Ford had long ago in his movements across the raw territories ceased to wonder. The struggle between mortal men and such country was a manifestly unequal one and Ford had sometimes marvelled at, sometimes held in contempt, those who persisted in their endeavours to hammer an existence from it. There were simpler, infinitely less-arduous, ways of making a living than pitting yourself against hell-holes like Baker's Creek.

He was kneeling among ancient boulders on a rise above Eder's, his horse picketed well out of sight in what passed for a cooler place, and he himself had been engaged for some twenty minutes in carrying out a painstaking inspection of the homestead and its surrounds, and he was close enough not to need his spyglass. The house was one which seemed to consist of about five rooms, perhaps a grander habitation in better times, but it was now old, its timbers curling; and it was adjoined by several lesser structures, one of which, the largest, was obviously a barn. There was a buckboard, down on one side, lacking one wheel, and what might once have been a chuck wagon, four-wheeled, with foot-high sides to it, a flat deck between, and some lockers. It might have been some time since the vehicle had seen either cook or range crew but unless closer inspection should disprove it, it appeared to be sound; which was more than could be said for Zachary Eder's spread in general. Beyond the barn there was a corral of sorts, but some of its poles had fallen. No horses were to be seen. There were horses down there though. Even as he had taken up his position, Ford had noticed someone moving around in the doorway of the barn, a man in a green shirt and a tall hat, a skinny man with the motions of a person of advancing age, whom Ford took to be Eder himself. This man had pushed open one of the tall doors of the barn and in the flood of sunlight Ford had glimpsed one horse, then become aware of another deeper inside the place. Two horses. Where there were two there could be a third. Eder seemed to be tipping grain into feed troughs and there was a certain amount of dust from it clouding the doorway. After a little time the thin man came out, pushed the barn door shut and walked across the dry yard to the house and went inside.

Ford slipped a silver watch from a fob pocket of his pants, glanced at it, snapped it shut, replaced it. It was much too early to move yet. Not until the sun passed behind the rims of the mountains would he venture closer, and even then, not until lamps had been lit and he could perhaps perceive movement through windows; and then he would come out of the darkness. And there were other, equally important, reasons for his attention to timing.

Not for the first time, as he waited, his thoughts turned to Ambler, and not for the first time he looked over his shoulder and made a careful examination of all the ravaged country at his back. The certain knowledge that this dangerous man was now in the town of Kellerman and had apparently shown not the slightest disposition to move on, was disturbing. It said that Ambler was not satisfied that the man he sought had moved away, and even though Ford could think of no trace that he might have left, sufficient to fuel Ambler's suspicions, he would be thankful nonetheless to get this present business over with, and leave. Had it been a matter of the bounty alone he might well have adopted a more prudent course and abandoned this particular task long ago. But it was not a matter of the bounty alone. He thought too, when he thought of Ambler in Kellerman, of trust and vulnerability. Undoubtedly a man was best alone, with no other tongue to wag; indeed it had been a policy that he had followed for nearly all of his early life, and of recent times he had ruminated over this at considerable length. To give due credit though, to have been quite alone out here, he might not so readily have become aware of Ambler. Perhaps that alone justified his present situation. No, there could be no gainsaying the fact that, with Frank Ambler on the scene, he needed resources more than he, just by himself, could provide. He dozed a little, came to full awareness again. It had been a long night but it had afforded him cover to visit Kellerman once more in the early hours, for a low-voiced, brief exchange out on the town's edge. The second attempt on Ambler had failed. Somebody else had been hit; that dumb ox from Massey's saloon who seemingly had come close to finishing Ambler himself. Ford swore softly. What a piece of luck that would have been. Ambler down an alley with his skull smashed in, and Eckhardt behind Ferron's bars, afterwards. On the debit side though, two bad mistakes, both caused by long shots, Ambler twice missed.

Satisfied that no other living thing was stirring under the pulsing heat of the afternoon and that the Eder place was standing peacefully, Ford withdrew into shade and sat propped against a rock, his long legs splayed out, even closing his eyes for a time and allowing his muscles to relax, husbanding his energy. Seldom at any time had he felt better than he did now, more in control of events.

* * *

Perkins, the doctor, had rooms above an assay office on Main; a pale-skinned, ginger-headed man with a blade of a nose and shrewd, bird-like eyes. His speech was crisp and he was forthright in manner and examined Ambler's puffed-up left hand with care and a surprising gentleness.

"Can't you move your fingers?"

Ambler concentrated. One by one he induced slight responses from each finger in turn.

"Um," said Perkins, taking hold of the wrist and holding the injured hand up, the better to observe it. "One thing for sure, I'll not be able to do much with it while that swelling is up." He poured cold water from a pitcher into a porcelain bowl and guided Ambler's hand into it. "Hold it in there for a while." After a few minutes he nodded and as Ambler lifted the dripping hand out, Perkins dried it by repeatedly dabbing a soft cloth on it. "That should be carried out a number of times in the next few hours. Cold water. It will help draw the bruising out and then the swelling should diminish." He fixed the bird-like eyes on his patient. "This would no doubt be the result of your argument with Mr Eckhardt?"

"The result of his attack on me," Ambler said quietly.

"Um. Yes. All right." Then, disregarding professional reticence, he said: "Mr Ferron is less than happy about all this."

"I am less than happy about all this," Ambler said, "but I didn't provoke Eckhardt or put the bullet in him. Ferron tells me it wasn't from a Colt."

Perkins pursed his lips, perhaps weighing the possibility of an answer against his ethics. Finally he said:

"In this part of the country, a man

doing what I do gets the task of taking bullets out of people more frequently than he would care to. After a while he develops a certain unwanted knowledge of bullets and what kind of gun might have fired them."

Ambler's interest sharpened though his hand now pained him more intensely than before.

"Do you have a theory about this bullet?"

For an answer Perkins turned to a shelf and brought from it a kidney dish.

"See for yourself, Mr Ambler."

The bullet which lay in the dish was partially flattened but enough of its original form remained for Ambler to see at once that it had not been fired from a Colt, just as Ferron had said. It was plain lead, hence its distortion on impact but its base had remained near to its shape when new, and it was of a much smaller calibre than Colt ammunition.

"I put a caliper on it," said Perkins,

now apparently relishing his role of expert. "I'd say it was European, quite small, eight-millimetre, no more."

"A foreign pistol?"

"There are a number of such weapons around, Mr Ambler."

"Can you guess the make?"

Perkins shook his head. "I'm afraid not, German, French, Russian. But a lot of those are eleven, twelve-millimetre." He paused and Ambler felt that the man still wanted to offer an opinion. "Um, I've even seen one or two of the latest French Army pistols; the Lebel, made in Saint Etienne." He shrugged as though to emphasize that it was a generalization and should be treated as such.

"Thanks anyway," said Ambler.

"Mr Ambler," said Perkins. "I am not a violent man but it has been my misfortune to observe a good deal of violence and to try to repair the worst effects of it. No violence is desirable, but I am particularly averse to those who are prepared to shoot at other human beings from cover or," and he blinked at Ambler who had the strong impression that the doctor was well acquainted with Ambler's reason for being in Kellerman at all, "or those who take the lives of others who are powerless to defend themselves. That is abhorrent to me."

Ambler stood up, nodded, and went out and down the narrow stairs to the street. His hand felt no better but he was pleased that he had taken Freda Shearman's advice and visited Perkins.

During the morning he treated his injury as the doctor had advised him to do and from time to time strolled out along Main, restless and wanting to be on the move. Once he thought he glimpsed Massey staring out at him across the batwing doors of the Silver Deck, but when he paused, the face, whoever it belonged to, withdrew. Ferron, he was aware, watched him from the window of his office, a cigar clamped in his teeth. And in the early afternoon he saw Cordry, mounted on a chestnut horse, jogging out of Kellerman just ahead of a single-horse buggy being driven by Freda Shearman. Though Ambler had thought about that attractive woman more than once, and while he had been aware of the spark of interest in her expression as she had talked with him, she merely provoked in him other thoughts, of the other honey-eyed girl, Emily Chater. The next time he returned to the hotel the desk clerk called to him and handed him a telegraph which had been sent care of the telegraph office in Kellerman and had been fetched along to the hotel. It was from Porter in Beauville. He thought that Ambler ought to know that the man Gemmel had a kinsman somewhere in the Kellerman area, someone by the name of Eder, last heard of at a place called Baker's Creek.

★ ★ ★

165

He had come upon them in almost complete silence after they had lit a lamp in the house.

"Where is it?" Ford asked in his hard voice.

"He cain't hear yuh!" said Gemmel, sweating, desperate.

Ford's expression did not alter one whit. It was as though he had turned to stone.

"I'll ask one more time," Ford said to Eder.

"He cain't — "

"Shut it!"

Eder looked from one to the other and his eyes seemed to grow bigger because it had now got through to him that something really bad was imminent. He was watching Ford the way he might have watched a swaying, venomous snake, and when he saw Ford's right thumb cock the hammer, Eder began to back off, thrusting the palms of his hands out, bumping against a chair in his retreat. Gemmel and Lowry began talking at the same time about Eder's inability to hear what Ford had been saying, but the gaunt, drably-dressed man told them to shut up unless they were going to say where the money was. When they fell silent and Eder found that he could back away no further because of the chair, which was solidly made, Ford spoke again.

"I ain't got time to piss about. This is the last time, the last chance he's got, deaf or dumb or whatever it is."

Eder's watery eyes had widened and he was swallowing hard, his attention shuttling from Ford to Gemmel to Lowry but he could draw nothing from any of them and his mouth fell open and his head began to wag from side to side and in the odd, high-pitched voice of a man deaf since birth he wheezed:

"Jim!" It sounded like "Yem!"

Ford extended his long right arm, presenting the pistol like a man at target practice. When, in the confines of the room, the weapon boomed, even Gemmel flinched; and Eder was thumped back right over the top of the chair as it too fell with the shock, and he slammed against the side of the stone chimney.

"God A'mighty!" shouted Gemmel. The room, in lamplight, was thick with gunsmoke and rank with the biting stench of burnt powder.

Eder was hit badly high up in his chest, hanging onto it with both hands and even trying to get up again, probably still numbed by the force of the bullet hitting him, with the pain yet to come. He did in fact get up as far as his knees before the strength left his legs and he slipped back and sat against the wall with his boots sticking out. The entire front of his shirt was now covered in blood and his hands were rich with it, hands which, after one final spasm from the body of Eder, fell away and lay limply on either side of him, palms upward.

Ford turned to Gemmel.

"Come on then. I told you there's no

time left to piss around. Where is it?"

Gemmel too was now shaking his head from side to side, his mouth working but no words coming. In a pinched voice it was Lowry who said:

"It's a long ways from here."

"Gemmel?" said Ford. "Where is it?"

Gemmel was breathing very short and his face was bright with sweat.

"Joe Half, he had it."

"You are a liar," Ford said, "and not even a good one."

"If he didn't have it when Porter took him, I don't know what he done with it."

"So you an' him," indicating Lowry, "just came right on down here without bothering any more about it," said Ford. "You are a liar. The Indian had nothing from Beauville. Neither of you would have trusted him for ten minutes with ten cents from Beauville." He wasted no more time but then with another deafening explosion clouded in smoke he shot Gemmel who went quick-pacing backwards with the impact until his boots went from under him and he fell full length, his spurs raking the floorboards and him beginning to shout in his pain.

"Oh Christ . . . A'mighty!"

Lowry's mouth was open, his eyes staring in utter disbelief. Gemmel was still thrashing, making noises as Ford then turned to Lowry who backed away until he was flat against the opposite wall. His glance, in desperation, flicked towards the door but Ford shook his head gently.

"Don't even let it come into your mind, boy. Now, this is the last time, just you an' me. Where is it?"

Gemmel shuddered and his fingers clawed up and he died. Perhaps Ford saw something in Lowry's eyes. Perhaps in his moment of extreme fear Lowry gave the slightest of hints, for Ford then said:

"So it is here. Well, it had to be. Whereabouts? Under here?" He tapped the floorboards with one toe, then nodded. "Under here. Get it."

Fifteen minutes later the canvas sack of money was out and the floorboards were nailed back into place. That was when Ford shot Lowry to death.

* * *

By nightfall, Ambler, still regularly immersing his left hand in cold water was still in some pain, though it had eased a little and he thought that the swelling had begun to diminish; but he could not yet close the hand into a fist. So he decided against setting out for Baker's Creek until sunup.

When that time arrived he was abroad early, and after he had eaten and, still with some difficulty, saddled up, he headed off along Main. Going by the jail he drew the horse to a halt and nodded to Ferron.

"Did you know that Gemmel has kin out here? At Baker's Creek?"

"Eder?" Ferron shook his head. "No notion o' that, Ambler, that connection.

171

None. Yuh go out there yuh'll need to shout. Zach Eder's stone deaf."

"If they're out there, those two, I won't need to shout," Ambler said.

"Yuh'll want to take some damn' care," Ferron said, "with two of 'em. If Ford ain't got there ahead of yuh, o' course. Anyway, it's Ford yuh want, ain't it?" He squinted at Ambler. "Yuh see sight or sound o' Cordry on the trail, tell him he'd best stir hisself an' git back here."

"I saw him leave, yesterday," said Ambler. "Where was he headed?"

"See a feller called Sholto about four mile this side o' the Kellerman. If yuh don't come on him afore the trail forks a couple o' mile from here, to git yuh to Baker's, yuh won't see him."

Ambler nodded, kneed the horse into motion.

By the time he turned off the Kellerman trail he had encountered no-one nor even sighted anyone in the distance. Moving away off the trail then to the left, seeing across a shifting haze the great curve of the Caber River, he began to come into rougher country. There was some relief as he drew nearer to the Caber, the land sloping down towards the water, but after he had slowly and with great care worked his way across the stone-rippling ford of the river, he moved closer in to the scarred northern reaches of the foothills of the Schaeffer Range. The going here was slow and the heat of the day was rising, beating down on him, Ambler was riding one-handed, the injured left one laid across his knee and he wondered if, in coming after Ford while still handicapped, he might not have made an ill-considered decision, one that he might yet live to regret.

Climbing to higher ground, reluctant to travel a trail capable of being overlooked by an enemy, going therefore across brushy slopes, he was keeping in view the glittering thread of Baker's Creek which eventually would go winding away across unappealing flats where Eder's place was, where either Lowry and Gemmel were, alive and confident in their bolt-hole, or gone, having been taken by Ford. These thoughts in his mind as he rode, he became suddenly aware that he was no longer alone. Around a clump of brush some two hundred yards ahead and slightly higher than Ambler, a horseman came into view. This other rider drew rein at precisely the same moment as did Ambler and the one sat staring towards the other across the baking distance between. There was something familiar about the horseman, Ambler thought. It was not Ford anyway, of that he was certain; then recognition came even as he started forward at a walk, the other doing likewise. It was Ferron's overdue deputy, Cordry.

Because of the nature of the footing in that place it was not possible to stop and converse except at a distance of some forty feet, but when they did, the sandy-headed man pushed back with one thumb his old, broad-brimmed hat, then sat unmoving, gloved hands resting on the saddle horn.

"Yuh're a good long ways out," said Cordry in his brittle voice, "on a day that ain't made for ridin' far."

"And so are you," Ambler observed, "and some distance off your trail, by Ferron's reckoning."

"Ah," said Cordry, his dark eyes unblinking, "yuh been talkin' to him."

"Him to me on that subject," Ambler said.

"There's more to this life than runnin' errands for the marshal," said Cordry, and gently touched the side of his nose with one finger and winked. "I got irons in fires all over."

"So it would appear," said Ambler. "Any of them happen to be anywhere around Eder's?"

"No. Eder wouldn't have been able to deliver what I wanted. You headed there?"

"Could be that I'll visit," said Ambler. "Passed anybody in the last hour?"

"Nobody. Christ, for a man with no warrant nor nothin' yuh got one hell of a lot o' questions, Ambler."

"I'm just naturally a man of questions. It's a fault. What about Ford? Have you seen Ford?"

"I ain't seen the bastard. I told yuh, I ain't seen nobody. Nobody apart from them I wanted to see." As he finished talking he took up the slack in the reins, indicating his readiness to move on. His intended path, Ambler saw, would take him somewhat higher than himself, up on his right hand side, and as Cordry's horse progressed, small runnels of stones began coming down; but Ambler had to take his attention off the Kellerman deputy and watch where his own mount was going. When he judged that, on his lower level he was well beyond Cordry, some inexplicable impulse caused him to glance back across the interval of still nearly forty feet separating him from the other rider. What he saw was incomprehensible, yet it was happening. Cordry's pistol was just then clearing leather and even as Ambler, abandoning caution, clapped spurs into the flanks of his own mount, the heavy thunder of the shot rolled down the hot dry slopes and a fire-rod laid itself across Ambler's back, on the left, two inches below his neck. He did not recall leaving the saddle but he was all too well aware of the shock to his left arm and leg as he struck the shaley slope and went sliding over a small bluff. The sound of the single shot was still rolling away, diminishing, and his horse, leaping in alarm across the uncertain ground was whickering, but Ambler was still sliding, then coming suddenly to a stop among clinging brush on the face of a slope.

Sodden with sweat, dust-covered, he lay there trying to take in draughts of air but it was air laden with white dust. His left hand hurt him badly, indeed his entire left arm ached, his hip bone had taken a heavy impact and the fire-rod was still across his back, but with a thick wetness now, his shirt sticking to it. He could hear but could not see a horse on the hill somewhere above him. The sounds seemed to be coming closer. No doubt this would be Cordry coming down to be sure he had made his kill. In the brief time left him to consider his situation and what if anything he could do about it, something else had at least come clear to Ambler. There was no doubt whatsoever now in his mind who it was who had made at least one of the attempts on him, in Kellerman; the first one it had been, the shot from the .45. But why Cordry? Maybe the answer to that lay in the fact that Ambler's information said that Ford had been in and out of Kellerman much more recently and more frequently than Ferron had said or maybe had known about. Cordry could have been Ford's ally for much longer than that. Once again the opinion of the Beauville peace officer, Porter, came back to him: "Don't be misled about Ford. People give out that because of what the man is, he's got no friends

178

at all . . . Sure, some o' them that Ford has might be such as don't want to wind up on the wrong side o' the man."

And when Ambler had estimated the kind of money Ford had picked up over recent years, when Ambler thought about it now, Ferron's surprise had seemed the more genuine. But of greater significance in the light of what was happening out here was Ambler's realization that it had been Cordry who had put in a most prompt appearance on both occasions in Kellerman when Ambler had been fired on. Indeed, the first time, he seemed to have come out of nowhere.

Small stones began running down the slope all around Ambler and dust was rising, but still he could see nothing of Cordry; yet neither, he believed, could he himself be seen among the brush. His hat had become dislodged so with his right hand he now carefully retrieved it from the interlaced branches. The worst thing, though, was that he did not know where his Colt pistol had gone. Perhaps in some reflex movement, as he had spilled from the saddle, he had begun to draw the weapon, and so had lost it; in any event it was no longer in its holster and from where he now lay he could not see it anywhere. Maybe it had slid further down.

There was no mistaking the sound now. Cordry was putting his horse down the slope, working among the brush, raising a good deal more dust while he was about it, coming to find his man, and when finally he did so, it would be all over quickly. Ambler forced himself to lie perfectly still, trying to ignore the running stones and choking dust. He thought that he had but one chance, albeit one so slim as to be scarcely worthy of the name, but it was all that he did have and, win or lose, he had no other course left open to him but to try it. On down came the mounted man amid his small, noisy avalanche, short-reined no doubt, the haunches of the animal nearly squatting, its forelegs thrusting stiffly, not liking this bad slope, Cordry having to give all his attention to staying in the saddle, fully committed now, and probably with the heavy pistol no longer held in one hand. When horse and man seemed poised right above the clump of brush where Ambler was, the man lying on the slope rose suddenly to his knees, then half stood, his big hat waving and Ambler letting rip a yell like some blood-mad Apache. Cordry's horse, already uneasy, now wide-eyed, screaming, rearing, twisting sideways, coming down on the slope all askew, was unmanageable, so its rider needed to get off it fast, he himself beginning to slide and flounder, his boots not made for such footing.

The horse, free of its burden, now partially recovered, got itself turned around and was trying to bound its way back up the slope to firmer ground; and as Cordry got up as far as his knees, also facing up the way he had come, Ambler was across to him. Cordry's

Colt was indeed back in its holster and when he dropped a hand to the butt of it and succeeded in pulling it clear, Ambler's right hand clamped on the wrist, forcing it wide of the other man's body. Ambler then pumped his right knee in under Cordry's ribs, producing a deep grunt of pain and then, locked together, they were rolling further down the rough slope, Cordry's pistol fallen somewhere, stones running afresh, dust rising. Cordry rolled on top of Ambler and scrabbled for a stone to strike him with but Ambler twisted aside, feeling a searing pain in his left hand as Cordry's weight came onto it, then lashed out with his right fist and had the satisfaction of catching the other in the left eye socket, jerking his head back; but Ambler knew it could not go on for long, that Cordry, with wiry strength and the use of both hands must eventually prevail.

Ambler saw his own pistol lying where it had slid to, further down the slope, even as Cordry began casting about for his. Ambler knew it was now or never and sprawled away, clutching for the weapon, having it slide from his sweating hand, then grasping it, rolling over even as Cordry, his Colt recovered, blasted a shot so close that it seemed Ambler would catch fire from it, but only small stones flew viciously and then the pistol in Ambler's own hand exploded almost under Cordry's jaw, blowing part of it away in a burst of red spray, a flicker of white bone; then Cordry was away and turning over twice, stopping on his back, legs quivering, sucking noises coming from his throat, arching, chest thrusting upwards, subsiding, dead, in his wreaths of dust and smoke.

Several minutes went by before Ambler could manage to move, to crawl down and look at Cordry. What remained of his mouth was open, a red-black cavern of blood and broken teeth, his eyes wide. Three or four yards away lay his blood-flecked hat. Ambler went through the pockets of the dead man; there were a few coins, several bills of small denomination and then a bundle of bills in a metal clip, these amounting to five hundred dollars. This would no doubt be from Ford in respect of services rendered. Dully, Ambler wondered if, at the first attempt on him outside the Alhambra Cordry had been successful, it might have been a thousand or even fifteen hundred.

It took him twenty minutes to climb back up to where he had sat his horse, talking with Cordry, and a further fifteen minutes calling and whistling, to find and secure the animal. Cordry's mount was way further up the slope, standing with its reins hanging. By and by it would find its way down to Baker's Creek; and the slim waterway was where Ambler went once he managed to get his aching body with its pain-pulsing left hand and arm, back on the horse. At the creek he got down stiffly, allowed the horse to drink, then with his one good hand stripped off his shirt, sloshed water over his face, head and upper body, trying without much success to get a look at the burning bullet-welt on his back. He splashed cold water on it, gritting his teeth at the pain it provoked. When he had finished and again slid into the shirt with the bloodied scar on its back, he had to decide whether he should go on or not. When finally he again got himself aboard the horse the desire to come up with Ford was the stronger and caution played no part in it.

There was a trail that followed the creek, the regular trail from Kellerman to Baker's which he had chosen to avoid earlier, favouring the more difficult but higher ground, wary of attack from above. Now that Cordry was gone, having been exposed as Ford's man, he no longer believed that Ford himself was in the vicinity.

From this point on he was able to make better time using this low trail, but it was past noon when he drew rein in the shelter of large rocks at a spot from which he could look down on

Eder's place, not knowing that it had been from this same one that Ford had done likewise only the day before.

The first thing that struck Ambler was the absolute stillness of the place, homestead, yard, outbuildings and corral; and beyond all those structures, across the brush-flats, only a few whorls of white dust were moving.

★ ★ ★

This morning, thought Ferron tetchily, folk seemed hell-bent upon bringing him trivia to deal with, taking up his already overtaxed time with it. He had been on his way back from one of the saloons having there delivered a stern warning about a dispute over cards which on the previous evening had led to a brawl involving several breakages and which had unsettled those of the townsfolk who had witnessed it. And now he was continually impeded during the walk back to the office by people who still wished to discuss other matters, such as complaints involving neighbours. He had managed to get as far as the boardwalk outside his own door, his face ruddy and his shirt already plastered to his back when he noticed a horseman in range clothing jogging into Kellerman and angling towards a two-storey building on the opposite side of Main. Ferron paused, looking at the newcomer speculatively as he dismounted and hitched his horse to one of the rails. Ferron nodded as the man glanced across the street in his direction, then, pausing to allow a buckboard to go rattling by, shoved his battered old hat to the back of his head and strolled across towards the Kellerman peace officer.

"Ferron."

"Sholto."

Ernie Sholto was a stringy, tough-looking man with a swarthy complexion and faded blue eyes, fans of wrinkles at their outer edges. Dressed in moleskin trousers he had on well worn, brush-scratched leather chaps over the top

187

of them and wore, too, a nearly-colourless, much-repaired denim shirt. Slung at his narrow middle with an ancient gunbelt he had only a half dozen spare loads gleaming brassily in it, and in an oil-blackened holster high up near his hip, a heavy Colt.

"Yuh look to be some flustered, Marshal," the rancher observed. Halting before Ferron he produced the makings and with slow deliberation began building a smoke.

"Yeah, well," said Ferron, "I got too much to do an' not enough help doin' it, an' that's a fact." He squinted at Sholto. "My deppity come out?"

"Yep," said Sholto, "that's why I'm in town."

"You an' Pearce settle the argument, then?"

Sholto struck a match on the sole of his boot and lit his skinny quirly, looking narrowly through the trails of blue smoke.

"Not yet, but it's headin' that way. Come in today special, to talk with that attorney, Phelps, draw up a proper water-rights agreement, once an' fer all, otherwise our kin might be arguin' into the next century, or worse."

Ferron nodded, thankful for what he perceived, on a bad day, as refreshing if unexpected evidence of sanity among men. Then he asked:

"What hour did Cordry leave your spread yesterday?"

"Leave?" Sholto spat out a stray remnant of tobacco. "Oh, he warn't out there long. No, not long at all. Four o'clock, mebbe, he pulled out. No later."

Ferron's clawed fingers scratched slowly at his middle.

"Four," He sniffed, patted a couple of pockets absently. "Cordry on his own?"

"On his own? Well, yeah, o' course he was on his own. Why?"

"Oh, nothin'," Ferron said. "There was a woman in a buggy headin' out to the Kellerman an' he was ridin' with her as far as your spread."

"Well," said Sholto, "she must've

drove on when they come to the fork in the trail. No buggy. No woman. Where is he?"

"If I knew that," said Ferron, "I wouldn't be askin' an' I wouldn't have all this here paperwork an' such, pilin' up. I'll boot the bastard's backside when he does show."

As a man whose daily problems included dealing with hired help, Sholto shook his head slowly, completely in accord with the marshal's mood.

When Sholto had walked away across the street Ferron went on inside his office and took off his hat and threw it on the floor. He thumbed a watch out of a fob pocket of his pants, looked at it, snapped it shut, put it away; then he retrieved his hat and walked out and around to the jail yard.

★ ★ ★

Ambler, aching all over, his left hand in particular still paining him badly, again unslung his canteen, took a drink, tipped some water over his face. He restored the canteen to its place on the horse and rubbed the animal's sleek neck for several seconds, then resumed his patient scrutiny of Eder's place which still stood silently in the hot sun. Not the merest movement had he seen down there but years of dangerous living and the innate caution that his hard life had produced in him, insisted that stillness did not necessarily mean that there was nobody down there. Again, just as Ford in his turn had done, he turned to examine all of the skyline behind him, then resumed his surveillance of Eder's.

The encounter with Cordry, its revelations and its outcome had shaken him. It was impossible for any man of character and some sensibilities not to be appalled by violent death no matter how hazardous his life, how hardening his experiences, how resolved he might see himself in seeking retribution. In a broader sense, all violent death diminished the living; humanity lost some fine part of itself. Those who were not revolted by it became, as Ford had done, in some way armoured against the effects of it, ultimately deadened in mind and spirit. Perhaps it was Ford's name entering his mind again that was sufficient to bestir him, for now he straightened, turned towards the horse and swung up into the saddle. Carefully he guided the animal out between the large rocks and headed it down the slope. Prudently he loosened the pistol in its holster but he did not draw it; his one good hand had to keep firm hold of the reins; but all the way down the tilted land, moving the horse at a walk, he held his attention firmly upon Eder's house.

Forty feet from the back porch he got down and allowed the horse to stand with reins hanging while he went forward on foot, the big pistol now drawn, cocked and canted skywards. He mounted the steps onto the porch and saw that the door was standing wide open. Ambler stepped inside.

* * *

It would be true to say that Marshal Ferron's feelings concerning the present whereabouts of his deputy alternated between extreme impatience and an odd, unnameable concern. Cordry's task, given him on the previous day by Ferron himself, had been to ride out to the Sholto ranch and convey to Sholto in person the marshal's word that a long-standing dispute over certain water rights between Sholto and a man called Pearce, must now be resolved without further delay, without acrimony upon either part and, most importantly, without any hint of violence. The fact that, apparently, a Mrs Shearman had declared her intention of driving out alone to the Kellerman Mine, there to meet her husband, and that Cordry, with some alacrity, had seemingly offered himself as escort as far as Sholto's, had been fine by Ferron, though he had made it perfectly clear to Cordry that nothing was to be allowed to deflect the deputy from his assigned task.

"Make damn' sure Sholto understands that my patience has plumb run out," Ferron had said. "I've already given Pearce my last word on it. I'll not be the mediator no more. Tell Sholto what I told Pearce. Fix it." Thus fully seized with the intent of his mission, Cordry had departed and Ferron had expected him to reappear in Kellerman if not late on that same evening, then certainly quite early the next day. Cordry had not come. Ferron had now made a decision, partly to separate himself from the irritating, petty affairs being imposed on him in town, partly to give Cordry a piece of his mind at the earliest possible time, to ride out and meet him on the trail. He saddled his horse, slipped his Winchester into its scabbard, locked the office and headed on out.

When, by the time he reached the Baker's Creek fork, he still could see no sign of Cordry's approach along

194

the trail towards Sholto's and the Kellerman Mine, Ferron hauled up and swore clearly several times. It was puzzling, frustrating. Cordry was certainly not coming from the direction from which he ought to be coming, nobody was, and while Cordry would have had no call to go along the Baker's Creek trail, Ferron could only think that for an unknown reason, he might have done. So he decided to ride along that way for maybe an hour and if there was still no sign of the deputy, turn around and go back to Kellerman. He forded the Cheyne River, then began ambling along the faint trail that more or less followed Baker's Creek, pausing once to refresh himself and his horse. Carrying on steadily, he had just fingered his watch out and looked at it and was about to turn the horse about and go back the way he had come when some distance up ahead he saw buzzards floating down. He drew rein, watching. They were not alighting on the trail itself but up on the dry brushy slopes up ahead and to his right. Ferron did not altogether fancy trying to coax the horse up there for the footing looked poor, but he concluded that he must try to find out what it was that was attracting the sombre birds.

He was right about the horse not liking the shaley incline and in fact, after the initial attempt, did not force the animal to go at it. Instead he hitched it to an arm of brush just off the trail and climbed up there afoot. Sweat was slick all over him by the time he achieved his purpose, he was plastered with fine dust and was gasping, waving his hat to cause the buzzards to rise again, reluctantly, to soar and wheel, not abandoning the place, prepared to wait for the intruder's departure. What he saw now near turned his stomach.

He had sure enough found Cordry. Incomprehensibly well out of his way, undeniably dead, half of his jaw and part of his head missing, the great wound black with a moving mass of flies, eyes already picked out by the death birds, and some other, unspeakable matter hauled partly out through one of the sockets. Ferron turned half away, swallowing hard, then stood drawing air deeply into his lungs, a new, oddly cold sweat on his forehead.

"Jesus!"

Breathing hard, he compelled himself to gather as many good-sized stones as he could, taking care not to tip off balance and go slipping down the slope, and with them built a mound over Cordry's ravaged head, then placed other stones over the rest of him. For some three quarters of an hour Ferron worked at this task and when, even his gloved fingers feeling bruised from handling the stones he had, after a fashion, covered Cordry, he sat down, his chest heaving, taking time in recovering, and glanced up at the blue vault of the sky with its half-dozen scavengers still wheeling lazily.

"Now do yore worst, yuh bastards."

He wondered if whoever it was had killed Cordry had also taken his horse for he could see no sign of it. When he had got his breathing under control and had got to his feet somewhat unsteadily and made his way down the slope again in short, staggering rushes, clutching sometimes at spiny brush, he made his way to the creek and for several minutes lay down in the barely-moving water. He was aching and shocked and confused, but after a while it came to him that if Cordry was out here, then he might have been going to or coming from Eder's place, and that was where Ambler had been heading, hoping to discover Ford. And like as not Lowry and Gemmel as well.

11

IN the kitchen one heavy chair was tipped over and there was a great deal of blood; it was on the floor, on the walls, even on the table, and there was a smear of it on one of the windows. Plainly, some kind of major slaughter had taken place in this room, and not too long ago; for although the blood had partly dried it could still be streaked with a finger; and there was the faint suggestion of burnt powder in the air.

Ambler stood still, surveying the scene. When he was satisfied that he had missed nothing, he walked slowly through the entire house, but entering each of the rooms with great care. In one room he discovered a large floor-to-ceiling cupboard and opened it gingerly but it contained only clothing and old boots. Ambler came back through into the kitchen.

There remained a number of out-buildings and the large barn. His first act, however, when he went back outside, was to fetch the horse across to the porch and hitch it to the railing. He rubbed the nose of the horse and then, moving as quietly as he could, began to search all of the out-buildings. The barn he left to the last, and even as he approached it, froze in his tracks as he heard from within the whickering of a horse. The tall doors of the barn had been pulled to but not quite closed. Ambler took a couple of quick paces to one side so that to anyone waiting inside the barn he would not be framed brightly in the gap between the doors. Often, a barn would have another, a single, smaller door somewhere and he made his way unhurriedly around the building until he found it. He was prepared to have to kick it in, but surprisingly, when he leaned across and lifted the latch, the door swung open.

Ambler went in fast, crouching, dodging down behind a stack of sacked grain, at once aware of the warm close atmosphere. There were chinks between the old boards, admitting bright shafts of sunlight in which myriads of dust-motes were moving. When his eyes became accustomed to the dimness, Ambler half rose from behind the sacks and saw that across on the other side of the wide building there were two horses standing near some feed troughs; and there was another trough, with water in it. There was a smallish mare and another, bigger animal, which obviously was a good quality saddle horse. One of the horses turned its head to look as Ambler walked across the straw-littered floor towards a fixed ladder leading to a loft. He had to holster the pistol and use his right hand, climbing up to look; but the loft contained only bales of straw. Ambler came down and went across to the horses. The mare had a KL brand which he judged to be the Kellerman livery mark, the other, a roan, a rough twin-diamond brand that was unfamiliar to him.

The only other thing inside Eder's barn was a small buggy. Ambler stood looking at it for quite some time, perhaps not wanting to admit the implications of what he was seeing; the mare and this buggy. In just such a vehicle, hired from the livery, Freda Shearman had driven out of Kellerman; and deputy marshal Cordry had been riding with her. Ambler's tongue ran between dry lips and he felt a weakness in his legs. It could not, must not be. But Cordry's dry-stick voice came back to him from the dead: ' . . . Eder wouldn't have been able to deliver what I wanted . . . ' A coldness now inside him, Ambler went to the main doors and pulled one of them open so that the horses would have freedom to come and go. He then got hold of a sack of feed and topped up the troughs. Outside in the yard again he looked at a vehicle he had noticed there earlier, a buckboard with one wheel missing.

Out on the other side of the yard, behind the barn, was a broken-down corral. The whole outfit told a story of disuse and indolence. He was just about to turn away when something else caught his attention. A few yards out from the corral there was an area of freshly-dug earth.

Dully, as from a sudden spasm of shock, his thoughts began to link together what he had seen in the barn with what he was now looking at; an area of turned ground that bore faint traces even now of discolouration from damp, as though in recent hours it might first have been thoroughly soaked with water to make it more easily workable. Knowing, with revulsion, what he must do, Ambler went across to a shed in which, earlier, he had noticed implements. As he reached in and took up a spade he saw nearby a pick-axe with traces of earth still adhering to it. Ambler carried the spade to the dug patch and began the task of uncovering whatever it was that might be buried there. He worked slowly for he was virtually still one-handed, therefore sometimes dragging away earth with his gloved right hand, for handling the spade was awkward, and probing with fingers, reluctant, anyway, to drive the spade down too hard. A good half hour went by and he had reached a depth of some three feet before his questing probe of fingers came against something other than earth, wielding, yet also resisting. Little by little removing more earth, he began to uncover the body.

A view of the face was enough, for whoever had done the burying had not troubled to cover it in any way and dirt was clogged in eyes, mouth and nostrils; but it was still plain to see that this was the face of a man in perhaps his sixties, narrow, sharply-boned, the hair grey and sparse. Ambler sat back for a moment or two on his haunches, knowing that he must be looking at the remains of Eder; and clearly there was no other body down here. His shirt rasping on the wound across his back, he began to cover the old man over again with earth. This killing would be Ford's work, Ambler had no doubt of it. Equally, he had no doubt that Gemmel and Lowry had been at this place and that somehow the bounty hunter had surprised them and shot them, else why dispose of old Eder too? But what then? Once more he put to himself the question: "What would Ford have done?" Well, he had not headed towards Kellerman or Ambler would have seen, if not encountered him; and anyway there was no reason at all for Ford to do so. Ferron could not have paid him his bounty. No, to get that, Ford would have had to set out on the long journey to Beauville, taking two dead men with him and, unless Ambler was much mistaken, taking the proceeds of the Beauville bank robbery as well, but not with the object of restoring it to its rightful owners; for there was no-one left alive who could have told where it was. Hidden in some place unknown, would no doubt be Ford's line. So when it was all done, it would have been a most lucrative campaign for Ford, and went a long way to explaining his persistence; all rewards and bounties outstanding for Gemmel and Lowry and the money from the bank on top. And a man already accustomed to money and working for more, and worthwhile money, had the where-withal not only to buy help but also to buy silence. The Eders of the world, however, would have no value in Ezra Ford's ledger and no significance in his scheme of things.

Yet one mystery remained. If Cordry had fetched Freda Shearman out here, what had been done with her? She was neither in the house nor any of the outbuildings, nor was she lying with poor old Eder in an oblong of his own sorry earth. It seemed inescapable that Ford had taken her. And whatever arrangements had been necessary to accomplish that as well as to transport two bodies all the long way to Beauville it seemed likely that something more than horses would be needed. Going over the yard, examining its surface, Ambler finally found what he had been seeking; in one place, not far beyond where the broken buckboard was, there were indentations indicating that a heavy vehicle had stood there for some while, then wheel marks leading away from that spot towards Baker's Creek; and there, quite clearly, he could see deeper ruts made by a four-wheeled wagon of some size that had been driven across. Obviously Ford was going for broke and had embarked on the long haul to Beauville, all his cargo in a wagon. It was like an echo of Cordry's crackling voice, in Ferron's office, about an earlier victim: "Stiff as a board. In a wagon." Such a thing meant, of course, that Ford's progress must be relatively slow for it would be a heavy rig, probably fitted with water casks and drawn by perhaps only two horses. Ambler went to his own horse and mounted up. He was now deeply concerned for Freda Shearman as well. If, a little time earlier, he had weighed the options of carrying on or of returning to Kellerman, and even though he was still in a poor condition, he now considered he had no choice; he must get out after Ford.

As he rode, going at a steady clip, weaving in and out between rocks and clumps of clawing brush, he was conscious of the fact that he was raising dust, but that could not be helped. To proceed more carefully meant that he would have to travel more slowly, and he was not prepared to allow Ford to get too far away. The image of the man as it had been revealed to him in the photograph at Emily Chater's house was still absolutely clear in his mind; the dark visage with the dark horseshoe of a drooping moustache, and the unusual, dark Amish hat. He would know Ford anywhere, of that he was certain.

The wagon had left a trail that

was quite clear in many places but that faded out when traversing harder ground. Occasionally losing sight of it for longer stretches than usual, because of such ground conditions, he had to make wide circles quite slowly, not worrying about time lost, in order to pick it up again. Yet he felt frustrated whenever this occurred and he did lose time, and as a consequence had to increase his pace over ground where the wheel tracks were plainly to be seen.

As he drove himself onwards under the hammering heat he was well aware that the country itself was becoming rougher. It was much more broken now, and there were many more upthrusts of rock and larger, and thicker, patches of brush, all of which would offer dangerous concealment for Ford should he become aware of pursuit and make the decision to wait and to stop his pursuer once and for all. There was nothing that Ambler could do about that except try to remain constantly alert, even to pause, himself, from time to time and study carefully the lie of the country up ahead; but the very nature of it rendered this a most difficult procedure. This was territory that he had no knowledge of, therefore he was unaware what habitations, if any, he might come upon; or worse, if he might at any moment encounter others who might be in Ford's debt to the extent that they, too, might try for Ambler so that Ford himself could run free. A man, thought Ambler again, who had the wherewithal to buy help. After the experience with Cordry, a town's deputy marshal no less, Ambler had come to believe that anything was possible.

★ ★ ★

Ford, for his part, believed that he had a sixth sense. Certainly, time and again he had demonstrated an uncanny ability to outguess men who had been his quarry; to appear suddenly, stunningly, when the odds were against his being closer to them than a hundred miles. The elusive, dangerous Kansan, Cayley, had been a case in point. Cayley had not had even the remotest notion that anyone else was anywhere near that range, let alone the brush-masked canyon, until the cold hard barrel of the pistol was laid against the corner of his mouth. In the low evening light the abandoned mine shack was gloomy and whoever it was who was holding the pistol was off to one side in shadow, only an indistinct shape; but the strange, rank smell of him was there all right, and when he spoke his voice was low but hard.

"Benjamin Cayley?"

Cayley had stood stock still the moment the steel had touched him and he found that his voice would not come easily, so he did not attempt to speak.

"Benjamin Cayley?"

When he had still made no response the man in the shadows had said:

"I won't ask a third time," and the

pistol was cocked.

"I'm Cayley."

"Now we're doing fine, boy."

"Who are you?"

"You can't ask that. You ain't holding the iron."

"What is it yuh want?"

"Want? I want you, Cayley. Well, that ain't quite true. I'm here on behalf of other people who want you."

"You the law?"

"No."

It had been about then that it had hit Cayley.

"Christ!"

"Not him, neither."

"Bounty!" Cayley had said. "Yuh're Ford!"

"Maybe. We'll see."

"How the hell did yuh know where I'd be? All the signs, all the word would say Balchin, or mebbe north o' Balchin."

"All the signs," Ford had said. "Signs mean nothing to me, boy. Right enough, I'm Ezra Ford. I *know*."

212

And now, the wagon standing below but out of sight, Ford propped one of his long, spidery legs against a boulder and stared through his glass back into the shimmering bars of heat that lay across the brush-riddled, stony land. He could at this moment discern nothing untoward, yet he *knew*. And if — no, *because* — someone would be coming, way back there somewhere, he also knew who it would be. It would be Frank Ambler. It was dust that he was looking for first. He even put the glass away and interlaced his long fingers, holding his hands up like that to extend the brim of his strange hat, offering more shade to his eyes, moving his upper body slowly left then slowly right. Still he could see no dust. No matter, from this time on he would check the back trail in this careful manner every ten minutes or so, and sooner or later, the dust would be there. Ford knew that there would be no point in trying to outrun the man who would be coming. Unless he became incapable of getting on a horse, someone like Frank Ambler would not abandon the chase. It was not in his nature.

For in Ford's mind there was no doubt, either, that by this time Ambler, building on bits and pieces of information and of discovery, would have pieced it all together — well, most of it. He was not a man to be under-estimated. Of course there was just a chance that he might have run into that vain fool, Cordry, somewhere along the way, and if a man could bring himself to believe, even for a moment, in miracles, Cordry might, just might, have stopped him. Even Ford could not deny himself a wintry smile as that particular fancy crossed his mind. Realistically he did not admit the notion of Cordry managing to get the better of a man like Ambler. So he must continue to assume that Ambler would be coming. Well, there was still an ace in the hole, and Ambler would discover the difference, if it had occurred, between dealing with some greedy, dim-witted deputy marshal *from* Hicksville and Ezra Ford. The Ezra Ford.

★ ★ ★

The further Ambler progressed the less did he like the look of the country he was moving into, a country filled with places made for ambush. For a time he had made every effort to keep to firmer ground in order to minimize rising dust but now, because it had had the effect of reducing his pace, he was simply pressing on, dust or no dust. Ford was no fool. He would know that Ambler was coming. A lot of dust or not much dust, Ford would be bound to see it for he would know, too, that Ambler, a man mounted, must be closing the distance between them. Ford would be checking his back trail quite often, perhaps at fifteen, maybe even ten-minute intervals, and from somewhere among the ugly rocks which proliferated out here. One thing that fell in Ambler's favour, something that he remembered from among the myriad scraps of information that he had collected, was that for some unknown reason, Ford seldom carried a rifle. So that was something.

Countless times, as he rode, Ambler had practised moving the fingers of his left hand, but hand and fingers were still puffy and he could not even nearly make a fist; the pain, however, had to some extent subsided. But the welt in his upper back still stung sharply.

Ambler pulled the horse to a halt. In coming around a clump of brush, faced with a stretch of comparatively open country which, in the distance, broke again into rocky passages, he was sure he had caught sight of a deeper smudge amid the shimmering haze of heat. He strained to make out what was causing it but it was too far off. Ford? Some other rider? Cattlemen? A whirl of richer dust, wind-driven? He did not think so. There was not enough wind in this searing oven, he thought, to whip up dust in that way. Only someone, something, on the move would be doing that. Ambler nudged the horse into motion again, not worrying now about wagon tracks or the intermittent lack of them, but heading directly towards the ephemeral smudge in the far distance, banking on its being produced by a wagon being driven by Ford with his cargo of dead. A few minutes later, the haze dancing before his eyes, he had lost it. He drew to a halt again, squinting into the glare. Nothing. He had not imagined it, become the victim of some aberration of light and sight, of that he felt certain. No, for there it was again, and plainer than ever. Ambler, relieved, began to go forward again at a steady pace. He was convinced now that it was indeed Ford, and that the short interval during which he had lost sight of the dust had been caused by Ford's coming to a brief stop, the better to view the back trail. Maybe he even had a glass. There would be no doubt about it now, anyway; Ford would know for sure that he was coming for him.

Distance, however, can be deceptive. For what Ambler regarded as a long while he seemed to be making little if any gain on his quarry, though there could be no doubt that he would be moving much more quickly than would Ford's wagon. At one particular place, however, his view was impeded by several large upthrusts of rock, and as he emerged, in firm going, between them, and beheld another long stretch of flats, he exulted when he saw not only dust up ahead but the clear shape of the wagon and a figure driving it. At one instant he thought he caught a lighter flash as though a face had turned to look back, and then he saw movement seemingly intensified as no doubt the horses were being whipped to greater effort.

Ambler wound the reins around the wrist of his injured hand and with the other, eased the heavy Colt in its holster. He found as he drew nearer that because of the wagon's trailing dust he had to edge the running horse a little to one side to keep out of the way of the choking cloud. Certainly the wagon had increased speed, cumbersome as it was, a chuck-wagon by the looks, and he could see the driver's arm rising and falling as the two-horse team was urged along, to what real purpose Ambler could not guess, for it must surely have been seen as inevitable that the horseman must soon come up with it. Yet the driver, not looking back now, continued an urgent flailing of the whip, and now Ambler, with much satisfaction, could see the dark jacket and, most telling of all, the black, stiff-brimmed Amish hat. Ford. On the wagon, near the back, was a substantial box of the kind often seen on range chuck-wagons, but beyond that, on the deck proper, there appeared to be a large canvas tarpaulin that was covering something else.

Now the rattling, dust-plumed vehicle

began to go down a slight decline, surging ahead, bumping over small stones in its path, and something hummed near Ambler even as he heard the bang of a shot, and he grabbed the reins with his right hand and swung the horse to one side, over to the left, so that in coming up with the wagon he would be riding alongside at a distance of a dozen feet, and if he hung back slightly, could make another shot, for Ford, an awkward proposition.

At that instant one of the wagon wheels struck some object, probably a bigger stone, and as he rode hard, moving up to come abreast of it, Ambler saw the whole outfit kick upwards, then fall back noisily, but no longer straight and level. It had slewed slightly to one side. It did not seem possible that so solid a vehicle would not simply slow down, recover and continue as before, but the driver seemed to lose control of the two-horse team and at the next moment the wagon found a softer patch of earth and lurched again, badly, and as Ambler watched, began to go over.

The shafts snapped like brittle sticks, flinging the horses down in a welter of whipping broken harness, lashing hooves, and dust. The noise of the wagon crashing onto its side and even sliding a few yards down the shallow decline, the bursting of the water cask on one side, was almost at once buried under another, more agonizing sound. One horse, snapped harness trailing, was scrambling to its feet but the other, still entangled and its back broken, was thrashing and screaming and kicking up more dust in its agony and its vain efforts to rise.

There was so much confusion, so much dust now, that Ambler at first could not see what had become of the driver. Water was spreading onto the hot earth from the broken cask, one horse had trotted off maybe thirty yards, the other, twisted pitifully, was still screaming and thrashing. Ambler had swung out in a wide arc and come to a stop, looking back at the tipped wagon, looking for a sign of Ford. Then he saw the figure huddled on the ground across on the other side of the wagon and slightly ahead of it. And half in, half out of the wagon was a stained tarpaulin with rope around it, wrapping some large bundle, the bodies of Lowry and Gemmel, no doubt. The Amish hat was lying a little distance away.

Ambler backed his horse off slightly, dismounted and went to its head, soothing it, for clearly it was unsettled by the noises being made by the animal that was injured. He left his own horse then, drew the long pistol and walked the sixty feet to the other and, placing the muzzle against its forehead, shot it. The animal's head flopped down, its big body shuddered, and flecks of foam started out from its mouth. The silence that ran on after the gunshot seemed uncanny. A film of dust still hung over the scene as Ambler began to walk in holding the pistol out in front, covering the fallen wagon driver. He knew when he was still five paces away that something was wrong beyond the fact that the body was lying quite still and in an oddly twisted attitude. It did not look like Ford. When he was two paces away he knew with certainty that it was not Ford. The dark jacket might have been Ford's and the distinctive hat lying a few yards away certainly would have been, and even at reasonably close quarters, Ambler had been deceived.

Her neck had been broken, her head was at an unnatural angle, and though she was dressed in levis as well as a man's denim shirt there could be no mistaking, now, the slim feminine shape, a woman taller than average, perhaps, though not as tall as Ford; Freda Shearman. On the ground nearby lay a pistol. It was smaller than a Colt, with a black metal finish and an etched wooden butt which was curved but did not widen towards its end. There was a screw eye in the end of the butt for a lanyard. A little over nine inches long, it was of a calibre much smaller than .45. A brass plate, oval in shape was let into the butt on the right hand side, and though he could not make out all of the lettering, 'St Etienne' was clear enough. So the doctor, Perkins, had been almost inspired when he had offered the possibility of a French revolver having been used in the second attempt on Ambler, perhaps a French army Lebel. He put it down.

Ambler was stunned by the discoveries, so much so that he had allowed his concentration to lapse, and now at a sound, as of a hoof striking a stone, spun on his heel, swinging the big pistol up.

Ford was there. He was sitting there on a roan horse almost side-on to Ambler, hatless, his thick black hair bunched at his neck, his downturned black moustache making his appearance unmistakable. His approach must have been slow and quiet, for, until the last moment, Ambler had not been aware of it; but Ford had come to a halt some eighty feet away and had not drawn the Colt which, Ambler could see, was holstered high under the left armpit in what looked like a specially-made harness. Ambler allowed his own pistol to swing down and hang by his side.

"Ford?"

The horseman nodded.

"You're Frank Ambler."

"Yes."

Ford made a very slight gesture with his left hand, still holding the reins with it. His voice was not loud but sharp in the still air and it carried to Ambler without difficulty.

"Is she dead?"

"She is."

Ford looked down and then up again. Ambler said:

"This wasn't what was supposed to happen."

"No."

"Who is — was she?"

"Freda Ford. My wife."

Ambler felt the shock of that pass right through him and saw how naïve he really had been, all through. But he said:

"I knew her as Freda Shearman."

"That was her name afore we wed."

"She had me fooled."

Ford nodded. "She was an actress, once."

Ambler could not but marvel at marriage between such disparate types, Ford and the woman who had been his wife, Ford in his rough, dirty clothes and with the strange smell he had, so they said, Freda Ford, soft wand-slim and yes, elegant. But he said:

"Where did Cordry come in?"

A wintry smile came, then faded.

"For the opportunity of personal gain. He is a mercenary man."

"He was. Cordry's dead."

Ford's dark eyebrows went up slightly and he pursed his lips.

"You?"

Ambler nodded.

"He couldn't even get that right," Ford said.

Ambler watched as the roan shifted

its feet and the tall man moved to soothe it, a seemingly incongruous gesture, his gentleness with the horse. Ambler said:

"You know why I've come."

"I'd be a fool to pretend otherwise. There are a lot of things you can't know, Ambler."

"There are a few I do know, and one in particular, and we have to finish that."

"I know it." He moved his head. "I'd like to see her."

"I'll not deny you that. Back off first."

Ford shuffled the roan backwards, not taking his eyes off Ambler for an instant, until he was more than a hundred feet away. Slowly Ambler walked to his own horse and swung up, still watching Ford. When he was settled he walked the horse away so as to give Ford plenty of room. When Ambler stopped, Ford walked his horse forward and approached the tipped-over wagon and, from then on, ignored

Ambler. Ford got down and Ambler could see his head and shoulders as he bent closely over the body of the woman and he remained in that attitude for several minutes.

Ambler thought about it all. It had come clearer for him now and he saw that in his zeal to come up with Ford and Ford knowing it, he had been easily outplayed by this man. Having listened to Porter's sensible cautions he had then permitted the urgency of the chase to take precedence and had all but over-reached himself. He realized now how well Ford had used the time of day, the glare of heat, the dust that marked his progress as plainly as it was possible to do it; two of them in the wagon for some while, Ford's horse hitched on behind, until Ford had been quite sure that Ambler was following like something else tied on behind the wagon. Then, Freda donning his jacket and hat, he had ridden off on the roan, in among rocks, waiting for the pursuer to go hastening by, his whole attention focused on the wagon and its driver. Ambler then wondered at what point, had the wagon not overturned, Ford would have emerged from behind him to make the kill. Perhaps he would never had known about it.

Ford was moving. Ambler stood in the stirrups the better to see what the man was doing, then sat down again. Ford was carefully drawing the body of the woman into the shade of the wagon and he seemed to be taking time in arranging her there and covering her face with something. He must have slipped the jacket off her for he himself was now wearing it. Then he walked across and picked up his own hat, slapped it against one of his skinny legs before putting it on. He walked back to the wagon. Ambler suddenly realized why. The Beauville money. He called out:

"Leave it where it is!"

Ford looked up, shrugged, then glanced around almost absently, as though wondering if there was anything he had forgotten to do. He returned to the roan horse and swung his long leg over and settled into the saddle and gently turned the animal until it was more or less facing in Ambler's direction. The Navy Colt was still visible under his left arm. He walked the horse forward a short way, then stopped again.

"She was a good woman," he said. "She did what she thought was right as far as we were concerned."

"Can't ask more," said Ambler, thinking that this gentle woman must also have made the second attempt on his own life, desperate to prevent him finding Ford. But he said: "I'm sorry it turned out the way it did, but you must both have known what the risks were."

"We knew the risks," said Ford, "and that was that."

After another short pause, Ambler said:

"It doesn't square anything. Not between us."

"Oh, I know that, boy. I know that."

"You were headed for Beauville?"

"Yeah. I'll still be headed there when we've got this done."

Ambler smiled faintly. Then:

"You didn't need to kill Eder."

"You weren't there," Ford said. "You don't know that."

"You've got the taste, Ford," said Ambler. "It's long ago ceased to mean anything to you. Some say it's more than that, that you've lost your nerve, can't take the chance that one of them will jump you and have more luck than Sprague did." He was sure that went home, for Ford's head lifted a fraction.

When Ford had stopped, the interval between them was about a hundred feet. If Ford had been affected by what Ambler had said, he recovered quickly.

"We'd best find out where all this nerve is then."

His knees moved and the roan began

to walk. Ambler stayed where he was. The long pistol was a weight to pull out and he preferred to concentrate only on that, for he respected Ford's ability to get the Navy Colt in his hand quite quickly with his high cross-draw, but the walking horse might just render that less easy. Ford had the reins shortened up in his left hand while his right, pale, long-fingered, was resting lightly on his right knee.

Ford's horse kept coming on placidly and Ambler was sitting still on his, waiting. Ambler centred his attention on Ford's face, watching his eyes and just peripherally aware of the horseman's hand still resting on his knee, and the butt of the Colt sometimes visible sometimes not beneath the loose jacket, as Ford's body moved with the walking of the horse. Ambler began to believe that Ford would never move, for the distance was closing, so much so that Ambler wound another turn of rein around his left wrist, wanting to be sure of having instant control of the horse when the gunfire started.

Still Ford came on but as he came it seemed to Ambler that he now leaned forward slightly, perhaps with the design of offering a more difficult target, and the angle of his approach altered ever so slightly so that he now presented marginally more of his left side to Ambler. When his move came Ambler did not at once recognize it for what it was. Ford's hand did not move up to the Colt but his right shoulder dropped and in the very next instant the right hand came into view holding the Lebel pistol that Freda Ford had had and that Ford must have pushed into the side of his boot. Ford's arm was well extended and he fired even as Ambler tugged the horse sideways and got hold of his own pistol out before it came clear, the hammer-blow of Ford's bullet hitting him punched Ambler backwards.

The horse snorted and reared as Ambler fired, though the firing of the shot owed as much to the shock of his being hit as it did to intent, and even as he fell from the horse he knew that he had not hit Ford. Yet Ford's horse, too, was skitter-stepping nervously, and it was this that gave Ambler the whisper of another chance. Though he struck the ground with jarring force he did manage to keep hold of the pistol, but in a wave of dizziness saw two images of the horseman thirty feet from him before they merged and there was Ford again, sharply clear, still exasperatedly trying to get the horse settled down. Ambler, hurt and bleeding, managed to raise the big pistol and, even as Ford fired again, Ambler also shot and was not sure whether or not he had nicked Ford; but the dark man, having missed Ambler, was now backing the agitated horse away, apparently not willing to come in on top of Ambler's gun even though his man was down and in bad shape. But Ford, seemingly dismayed at missing Ambler with his second shot, the one that ought to have been the kill, had thrust the Lebel into his waistband and was now drawing the Navy Colt, the gun he was accustomed to. Ambler's horse had trotted off to one side and stopped. Ambler himself was trying to stand up, to get himself further away from Ford, but was not making much of a fist of it. He had managed to retreat only a couple of yards when he went down again. He had left a trail of blood, his entire left side was pulsing with pain and his vision was no longer clear. The long pistol seemed to have increased in weight and it was all he could do to keep a firm hold of it, let alone lift it for another shot at Ford.

Dimly he became aware that Ford's horse was again on the move, but try as he might he could not rise to defend himself. Ford was approaching, the Colt in his hand chopping downward, but even as he did so, his long, lean body was actually plucked from the saddle, or so Ambler thought, as though by some sudden, freak gust of wind, and

Ambler, muddled, mystified, heard the lashing sound of a shot that was not from a Colt. Ford's horse was galloping away, reins flying loose, and Ford himself was on the ground, covered in dust, his strange hat bowling away. Ambler could not make out whether or not the dark man was still holding onto his gun, nor for that matter understand why he was on the ground at all. Everything was fading.

Water slopping on his face brought another face to him, looking down; Ferron's. Now he was giving Ambler a drink from a canteen. Some of the water ran out of the corners of Ambler's mouth.

"Lie still," Ferron said. "I got to find somethin' to stop the blood." He was gone for some minutes, for he had to get to Ford's horse and manage to catch hold of the trailing reins. He led the animal nearer to where Ambler was and from it took down Ford's warbag. He found in it a couple of shirts which he tore up and used to wad against

Ambler's nasty wound, under the ribs on his left side. From the body of Ford he then removed the elaborate gun harness and used it to secure the padding.

"Ford . . . " Ambler began.

"Ford's dead." Ferron reached back, then held up his rifle. "Just as well I fetched it. Just as well for you. Now listen, this is one hell of a place to be, the shape yuh're in, Ambler. Yuh can't stay out here. After sundown, when the heat goes, we'd best hope for a good moon, try to get yuh to sit on the horse an' stay there, an' get back, nice an' easy, to Eder's. Yuh can wait there while I go back to Kellerman to fetch Perkins out."

"Gemmel and Lowry are at the wagon," Ambler muttered, "and there's a dead woman there. Freda Ford. His wife."

"Jesus," Ferron said.

A faint breeze had come up, but it was not a cooling breeze. White dust began to cover the dark clothing of

Ford, and filmed over the upturned wagon and the dead there. Ambler's breathing was laboured but he managed to ask:

"Did you find Cordry?"

"I found the buzzards first," said Ferron.

So that there could be no possible misunderstanding, Ambler said:

"Ford paid him. I shot him."

Ferron stared at Ambler for some seconds, then he stood up, his knee joints cracking. There were wheres and whyfors and all manner of other things in his mind but they would have to wait.

"I'm gonna try an' get yuh up on that horse," he said. "It might take a while."

12

TEN days had passed before he was able to walk any distance. The bullet had still been in him and Perkins had had some difficulty in getting it out without unduly carving him up. Now, still firmly strapped beneath his shirt, sitting in a chair in the office of the Kellerman marshal, Ambler watched as Ferron moved around with apparent aimlessness. Then, unexpectedly, the marshal produced from a cupboard a bottle of whiskey. A moment or two before that, he had found two shot glasses which then, inexplicably, he had put into a drawer; now he glanced around for them vaguely, once even patting his pockets. He then located the glasses in the drawer and set them out on his dirty old desk.

Ambler raised his drink to Ferron.

"Here's to chance," he said.

"To chance," said Ferron.

They had had plenty of discussion since the shooting of Ford. The Kellerman bank had arranged the conveyance of money to the bank at Beauville. All rewards and bounties, upon Ferron's personal guarantee that both Lowry and Gemmel were indeed dead and had been buried by a Kellerman party some miles north of Baker's Creek, were payable to Ferron himself, since Ambler had declined them and had held that, had it not been for Ferron, it might never have been known what had become of any of them. The Fords, man and wife, The Death Man and his bride, were out there too, on the arid flats, together in death.

Ambler had however, never quite got around to asking what he asked now.

"What made you come out to Eder's, just following the tracks, all that way?"

"Well," said Ferron, "it wasn't a case of jurisdiction nor nothin', for that far out from Kellerman, that don't mean a spit in hell. No, it was Cordry; the business about Cordry done it. I didn't know what he'd been up to out there, but he was shot dead an' he was my deputy, an' not too bad a one as all that, or so I thought, though I never did say so to him. I reckoned it had to be down to them two bastards. I hadn't counted Ford in it. Nor you. I was some riled up, kinda got carried away. Funny the way some things work out."

Ambler took a sip of his drink. He could have used some water in it but kept quiet for he felt that Ferron might not immediately remember where it was.

"I came all that way for Ford," Ambler said, "and in the finish I didn't get him. I've taken more difficult men than Ford. Maybe I'm past it. I told Ford he was. But I was taken in by those in his pay and by Freda, and probably lied to by any number of others for various reasons. I was out-thought by Ford, and finally out-fought by him as well. For a man supposed to be past it, he wasn't doing badly."

"Over the years," said Ferron, "I heard all sorts about the man, a lot of it no doubt hogwash. I even heard he was once well respected."

"I could believe it," said Ambler. "But something happened to Ford. Too much killing, fear for his own safety; fear for her, maybe, in years to come. Dead or alive. Dead was safer, on the journey in."

Ferron poured another shot. Ambler covered his glass, which still had some drink in it, shook his head.

"What will yuh do now?"

"It's uncertain," Ambler said. "I've got a particular place to go, somebody particular to see. It's uncertain, chancy; but I can't make other plans until I've tried."

Ferron raised his shot glass.

"Then here's to chance."

"I'll drink to that," said Ambler.

FIGHTING RAMROD
Charles N. Heckelmann

Most men would have cut their losses, but Frazer counted the bullets in his guns and said he'd soak the range in blood before he'd give up another inch of what was his.

LONE GUN
Eric Allen

Smoke Blackbird had been away too long. The Lequires had seized the Blackbird farm, forcing the Indians and settlers off, and no one seemed willing to fight! He had to fight alone.

THE THIRD RIDER
Barry Cord

Mel Rawlins wasn't going to let anything stand in his way. His father was murdered, his two brothers gone. Now Mel rode for vengeance.

ARIZONA DRIFTERS
W. C. Tuttle

When drifting Dutton and Lonnie Steelman decide to become partners they find that they have a common enemy in the formidable Thurston brothers.

TOMBSTONE
Matt Braun

Wells Fargo paid Luke Starbuck to outgun the silver-thieving stagecoach gang at Tombstone. Before long Luke can see the only thing bearing fruit in this eldorado will be the gallows tree.

HIGH BORDER RIDERS
Lee Floren

Buckshot McKee and Tortilla Joe cut the trail of a border tough who was running Mexican beef into Texas. They stopped the smuggler in his tracks.

BRETT RANDALL, GAMBLER
E. B. Mann

Larry Day had the choice of running away from the law or of assuming a dead man's place. No matter what he decided he was bound to end up dead.

THE GUNSHARP
William R. Cox

The Eggerleys weren't very smart. They trained their sights on Will Carney and Arizona's biggest blood bath began.

THE DEPUTY OF SAN RIANO
Lawrence A. Keating and
Al. P. Nelson

When a man fell dead from his horse, Ed Grant was spotted riding away from the scene. The deputy sheriff rode out after him and came up against everything from gunfire to dynamite.

HELL RIDERS
Steve Mensing

Wade Walker's kid brother, Duane, was locked up in the Silver City jail facing a rope at dawn. Wade was a ruthless outlaw, but he was smart, and he had vowed to have his brother out of jail before morning!

DESERT OF THE DAMNED
Nelson Nye

The law was after him for the murder of a marshal — a murder he didn't commit. Breen was after him for revenge — and Breen wouldn't stop at anything . . . blackmail, a frameup . . . or murder.

DAY OF THE COMANCHEROS
Steven C. Lawrence

Their very name struck terror into men's hearts — the Comancheros, a savage army of cutthroats who swept across Texas, leaving behind a bloodstained trail of robbery and murder.

SUNDANCE: SILENT ENEMY
John Benteen

A lone crazed Cheyenne was on a personal war path. They needed to pit one man against one crazed Indian. That man was Sundance.

LASSITER
Jack Slade

Lassiter wasn't the kind of man to listen to reason. Cross him once and he'll hold a grudge for years to come — if he let you live that long.

LAST STAGE TO GOMORRAH
Barry Cord

Jeff Carter, tough ex-riverboat gambler, now had himself a horse ranch that kept him free from gunfights and card games. Until Sturvesant of Wells Fargo showed up.